As Xandros's eyes rested on Rosalie, on her agitated, stricken face that, for all the emotion working in it, was still not diminished in its effect on him, on the emotion flashing in her eyes, lighting them up in a blaze, he heard the words rise up in his throat. Heard himself say them, insane, surely, as he was to say them...

And then he said them anyway.

"What if—" his eyes held hers, holding them by the sheer power of his will, which was welling up in him from that deep, impossible place in his brain "—there were a different alternative?"

She stared. Blankness was on her face now.

"What alternative?"

He held her eyes still—those beautiful, expressive eyes of hers—his expression masked. But beneath the mask his thoughts were racing. Was he really going to say what he was about to say? Could he really mean it?

Then there was no more time for questioning himself, for he could hear himself speak.

"You marry me after all."

Julia James lives in England and adores the peaceful verdant countryside and the wild shores of Cornwall. She also loves the Mediterranean—so rich in myth and history, with its sunbaked landscapes and olive groves, ancient ruins and azure seas. "The perfect setting for romance!" she says. "Rivaled only by the lush tropical heat of the Caribbean—palms swaying by a silver-sand beach lapped by turquoise waters... What more could lovers want?"

Books by Julia James

Harlequin Presents

A Cinderella for the Greek
Tycoon's Ring of Convenience
Billionaire's Mediterranean Proposal
Irresistible Bargain with the Greek
The Greek's Duty-Bound Royal Bride

Secret Heirs of Billionaires

The Greek's Secret Son

Mistress to Wife

Claiming His Scandalous Love-Child
Carrying His Scandalous Heir

One Night With Consequences

Heiress's Pregnancy Scandal

Visit the Author Profile page
at Harlequin.com for more titles.

Julia James

THE GREEK'S PENNILESS CINDERELLA

HARLEQUIN®
PRESENTS®

Recycling programs for this product may not exist in your area.

ISBN-13: 978-1-335-14882-7

The Greek's Penniless Cinderella

This edition published by arrangement with Harlequin Books S.A.

For questions and comments about the quality of this book, please contact us at CustomerService@Harlequin.com.

Harlequin Enterprises ULC
22 Adelaide St. West, 40th Floor
Toronto, Ontario M5H 4E3, Canada
www.Harlequin.com

Printed in U.S.A.

THE GREEK'S PENNILESS CINDERELLA

For Franny—my dearest friend. Always.

PROLOGUE

XANDROS LAKARIS TURNED ABRUPTLY, winged brows snapping together over his dark eyes, deepening the lines around his well-shaped mouth.

'Dammit! Just what do you suggest I do? Storm after her and drag her to the altar?' he demanded rhetorically.

The man he'd addressed, Stavros Coustakis, sat back in his chair, eyeing his visitor impassively. He had grey-green eyes, unusual for a Greek—but then—unlike Xandros, with his long and illustrious family history—Stavros Coustakis knew little about his antecedents.

'I'm a nobody,' he'd readily admitted, with the worldly cynicism Xandros was well used to in this man whose daughter he'd been engaged to marry, 'but I've made myself a very, very rich one.'

Those grey-green eyes hardened now at Xandros's outburst.

'No,' he retorted. 'It would do you no good. She has defied me and is therefore no longer my daughter.'

Xandros looked at him askance, his frown deepening. He knew Stavros was ruthless—a man few, if any, cared for—yet to hear him disown his daughter so casually was chilling. But he also knew that his own reaction to his former fiancée's flight was, in fact, predominantly relief.

He had been in no rush to abandon his carefree bachelor lifestyle, indulging in the easy-going short-term affairs which—thanks to his dark good looks, wealth and elevated social position in Athens society—had always come easily to him. Still only in his early thirties, he wanted a few more years of it before he tied himself down in marriage.

It was a preference which he knew warred with the dual responsibility pressing heavily on his shoulders—not only to continue the ancient Lakaris family line, which could trace its heritage back to the imperial nobility of the long-vanished Byzantine empire, but also everything his father had impressed upon him all his life. That old money must continually be replenished with new or risk disappearing completely.

It was that necessity which had dominated Xandros's childhood. His grandfather had fatally combined lavish spending with rash investments, and the family had come dangerously near the point of complete ruin because of it.

Financial worries had been paramount in his boyhood years, with his father plagued by unpaid creditors and even impending bankruptcy, his mother fearful that their beautiful, gracious family home in the countryside beyond Athens would have to be sold. His father had driven himself relentlessly to restore the Lakaris fortunes and reverse his own father's unwise profligacy.

He had succeeded more than handsomely, restoring the Lakaris fortunes by the time his son had reached adulthood, but Xandros had grown up indelibly imprinted with the task of continuing his father's work and ensuring that never again would they want for money—that the family's wealth would never again be endangered, only enlarged.

An ideal opportunity to do just that—hugely—had presented itself in the prospect of undertaking a highly mutually lucrative merger with the Coustakis empire, its financial lines of business, from venture capital to insurance, that would fit ideally with the Lakaris portfolio.

Xandros's father, before his untimely death, had been keen to press ahead with it—and not just for financial reasons alone.

Xandros was well aware that his late father had been very keen on pointing out that their ties with Coustakis could, and indeed should, be even closer. And that Stavros's daughter Ariadne, despite her father's rough-and-ready self-made origins, would, in all respects, make Xandros a highly suitable wife…

He could see why. Ariadne, though perhaps a little young for him, being only in her early twenties, ticked all the boxes. A striking brunette, intelligent and cultured, she socialised in the same elite circles as he did, and they got on perfectly well together. From his parents' point of view Ariadne had the added advantage of not only being Stavros Coustakis's heir, but also the fact that her late mother had come from a very good family and had been best friends with Xandros's mother.

Moreover, Stavros Coustakis himself had become very keen on making the proposed business deal much more than a corporate merger.

'I've a mind to be father-in-law to a Lakaris and have a Lakaris grandchild,' he'd informed Xandros bluntly. *'Being a nobody myself.'*

For all his late father's enthusiasm, and his mother's urging, it had still not been an easy decision for Xandros to make, but in the end he'd gone for it.

And so, he'd thought, had Ariadne, who was keen to escape her domineering father as much as having any desire to marry. Okay, so neither of them was in love with the other, but they liked each other well enough, and he'd determined to do his best to be a loyal and supportive husband, and eventually a loving father to their children. That would have been enough, wouldn't it?

Except the text he'd received that afternoon, making him rush hotfoot here to Stavros's showy mansion in an exclusive suburb of Athens, had disabused him of that assumption.

Xandros—I can't marry you after all. I'm leaving Athens. I'm sorry—Ariadne.

The words echoed again in his head now—as did the covert tug of relief that had sprung up in him as he'd taken in the implications of her rejection. With Ariadne removing herself from the frame, he was now free to make what he'd preferred all along—a marriage-free merger with Coustakis Corp.

He'd said as much to the man who was not, after all, going to be his father-in-law.

'Very well,' he said coolly now, his voice clipped. 'Then that is that. Ariadne is no longer in the equation. However, as I have argued from the outset, marrying your daughter was never essential to our merger.'

He kept his eyes levelled on Stavros, seated at his heavily gilded desk, aware that he wanted out of this oppressively over-opulent mansion as soon as possible.

His own taste was for minimalism, as in his own city apartment, or better still, the simplicity of his white-washed, blue-shuttered villa on Kallistris.

Kallistris! The very name could lift his spirits! His own private island—his haven—a helicopter flight from Athens. The place he escaped to whenever his work or social life permitted. He had purchased it on attaining his majority, knowing that it would always be a safe haven for him, whatever life threw at him.

He would fly out there this very evening—spend the weekend, get away from all this. Away from a man he didn't like, whose daughter he hadn't really wanted to marry and now didn't have to, because it seemed she hadn't wanted to marry him either. Stavros Coustakis could forget about his ambitions for a Lakaris son-in-law and grandchild. It wasn't going to happen.

But first he wanted a definitive answer on the one thing he *did* want—the merger he sought. His eyes rested on Stavros Coustakis now, as he waited for his reaction. Was it go or no go with the merger? He disliked being played—and with a party like Coustakis it was essential to meet hardball with hardball.

'You'll need to give me an agreement in principle,' he said now, 'or not.'

He glanced at his watch—a calculated hustle, as he well knew, and Coustakis would know, too, but that was the way the game was played.

'I'm flying out to Kallistris this evening.'

He wanted to be there in time to watch the sun set into the bay, the moon rise over the headland…

His mind snapped back to where he was now, and his gaze fixed on Stavros. Something was changing in those pouched grey-green eyes—they held a caustic gleam that Xandros suddenly did not like.

'I'm sorry to hear that,' Stavros was saying. His tone was smooth—too smooth. 'You see…'

There was a definite challenge in his voice now, which Xandros liked even less.

'Since you are so keen on this merger to take place, I had hoped that you would be flying to London instead.'

He smiled. Not a nice smile at all. And every particle of Xandros's consciousness went on high alert.

'In order to collect…' Stavros Coustakis's smile deepened, and the smile was indisputably a taunt, just as the now blatant cynical amusement in his eyes was overwhelmingly provocative '…my *other* daughter.'

Xandros froze.

CHAPTER ONE

ROSALIE SIGHED, CROUCHING down beside her bucket of soapy water, a heavy-duty scourer in her rubber-gloved hand, and poured bleach over the disgusting, greasy, trodden-in gunk on the cheap vinyl floor in front of the equally disgusting grease-splattered cooker.

The rest of the kitchen was just as disgusting. Whoever had rented this house had been a pig. The whole place was filthy, from top to bottom, and cleaning it was a pig as well. But it had to be done.

She sighed again. Her rent was due, and she also liked to eat.

She felt a familiar emotion burn in her.

One day I won't be doing this! One day I won't be cleaning up other people's filth and dirt! One day I won't be living in a total dive and paying a fortune for the privilege! One day I won't have a wardrobe consisting of clothes from charity shops! One day I won't be never going out and living on beans on toast...

One day she wouldn't be poor any more.

It was a poverty she'd grown up with. Her single mother, raising her daughter on benefits, had been plagued by lifelong ill health, and Rosalie had been her carer both as a child and into her twenties. She had never been able to make a life of her own. It had just been her and her poor, frail mum, living in a shabby council flat in the East End of London.

As for her father—he didn't even know she existed. Her mother had told her as much, sighing over the one all too brief romance in her sad life.

'I knew him for such a short time! He was foreign—so romantic!—working here in London on a construction site. Then I found I was pregnant, but he'd already left the country. I wrote to the construction company, to tell him you were on the way, but they couldn't have been able to trace him because I didn't hear back...'

And she never had either. Rosalie had written him off from an early age. All she and her mother had had was each other.

Rosalie's face shadowed. And now she did not even have her mother. Her poor unhappy mother had finally succumbed to chronic lung disease in the chill grip of last winter. With her death Rosalie had lost the council flat and lost the disability and carer's benefits she and her mother had lived on. But she had, she knew, gained her freedom.

Grieve though she did for her mother, she knew that finally, at twenty-six, she could belatedly start to make a life of her own. Make something of herself. Get qualifications, the ability to better herself, and escape from the poverty trap and the bleak, unlovely streets of her rundown part of the East End.

She sighed once more, scouring away at the filthy floor, feeling the small of her back aching. She'd been cleaning since eight in the morning, and now it was gone four. It would be another good hour's work on the kitchen before she could lock up, hand the key in to the agency, then get back to her poky bedsit and her crucial, all-important studies.

She'd signed up for online classes in accountancy, and getting those vital qualifications was her exit route out of poverty. To pay for them, and to pay for her dump of a bedsit and to keep body and soul together while she studied, she did cleaning work all day—however exhausting.

With a jerky movement she got to her feet, tipping the dirty water down the sink and setting it to refill, pouring in fresh bleach. She fetched the mop to clean the rest of the floor, then frowned suddenly, turning off the water as she hefted the full bucket.

What was that she'd heard?

The sound came again and she realised what it was. The doorbell was ringing.

Still frowning, and wary, for this low-rent house was not in the most salubrious area, she went into the entrance hall, setting down her bucket and opening the door cautiously. The view out to the nondescript street was almost completely blocked by the tall, male figure standing there.

Rosalie's eyes widened totally as impressions tumbled through her head. *Tall, dark hair, incredible eyes and face...*

Who on earth…?

She gulped silently, her gaze fastened on him helplessly. Then, abruptly, the man was speaking.

'I'm looking for Rosalie Jones,' he said, and his voice was deep and clipped and curt, with an accent she could not identify and had no time to think about.

Rosalie stared, still fixated on the overwhelming

visual impact the man standing there was having on her. Then she realised what he'd just said.

'Who wants to know?' she asked sharply.

Apprehension spiked in her. No one who looked like the man standing there could possibly have the slightest business being in a rundown area like this! Everything about him was wrong here.

It wasn't his foreignness—that was commonplace in London. She gave a silent gulp. It was that air of being from a different world altogether—smooth, urbane, cosmopolitan, sophisticated. A world of luxury and wealth…

The flash suit, the silk tie, the polished shoes, the gold pin on his tie...all wrong for this part of London...

And most of all it was wrong—totally wrong—that a man like that should be asking for *her*…

His expression had tightened, as if he wasn't used to being challenged in any way.

'I need to talk to her.' His reply ignored her demand. He merely sounded impatient at her delaying tactic. 'Is she here?'

Rosalie's grip on the door tightened. 'I'm Rosalie Jones,' she said. She spoke reluctantly, and was about to repeat her question as to who wanted to know, but the expression on the man's face had changed.

'You?' he said.

There was total disbelief in his voice.

The dark eyes skewered hers. '*You* are Rosalie Jones?' His mouth tightened to a thin line. 'Impossible,' he said.

For a moment he just stared at her, that look of disbelief still upon his ludicrously good-looking face, and Rosalie found herself going ramrod stiff at the way he was looking at her. Because there was more than just disbelief in his face… There was something that suddenly made her burningly conscious of the way she was looking. Of what he was seeing.

Me, looking a total fright after cleaning this pigsty all day...

Then, suddenly, he stepped indoors, and another spike of apprehension shot through her, cutting off that burning self-consciousness.

'What the—?' she began indignantly.

But he had closed the front door, turning to her. That look of disbelief was still on his face, but he was modifying it, she could tell. Now it was a grim look, as though he were steeling himself to talk to her.

'*You* are Rosalie Jones?' he echoed. Incredulity flattened his voice.

She stared. Why did he sound disbelieving?

She tilted her face—he seemed very tall and overpowering in the small hallway, which was ill lit and shadowed now that the front door to the street was closed. It made her supremely conscious of the visceral impact of the man, from his immaculately cut sable hair to his polished handmade shoes, via his planed and outrageously magnetic good looks and those amazing long-lashed dark eyes, which were raking over her as if he found her assertion outrageous.

'Yes,' she ground out again. And this time she got out the question *she* needed to ask—right now! 'Who are *you*, and what can you possibly want with me?' she threw at him.

With a visible tightening of his mouth, he answered her. 'My name is Alexandros Lakaris, and I am here because of your father,' he said.

* * *

Xandros saw the girl's expression go blank—and then pale with shock. His own feeling was not dissimilar, and had been ever since Stavros Coustakis had dropped his bombshell.

He could still hear the man's voice echoing in his head, and the exchange that had followed.

'Your other daughter?'

Xandros's stupefied repetition of what Stavros had announced had fallen from his lips and the older man's expression had not changed.

'Yes. I have another daughter. She lives in London. I am expecting you to go there and bring her here.'

He'd paused, and that unholy glint had come into his eyes again.

'Assuming, of course, you still wish to proceed with the merger you are so set on...'

Xandros's face had tightened, as if turning to set plaster.

'Tell me a little more, if you please, Stavros,' he'd replied.

His voice had been neutral...unlike the emotion scything in his chest. But he had determined he would deal with those emotions later. At that moment he'd simply needed information.

Stavros had supplied it, still speaking in that deliberately unconcerned way that Xandros had known was a wind-up—one he was equally determined not to react to.

'Her name is Rosalie Jones. She lives with her mother...or did until recently. I knew her mother...let me see, now...over twenty-five years ago, when I was working in the UK. It was a fleeting affair and we went

our separate ways. However, I have always known of my daughter's existence, and now I think it is time she came here to Athens.'

He'd smiled, and Xandros had not cared for that smile with every atom of his being.

'In order to replace my errant former daughter, Ariadne.'

He had smiled again—that same mocking smile.

'I look forward to her arrival.'

And that had been all Xandros had got from the man. That and the knowledge, both galling and enraging, that he had been both outplayed and outmanoeuvred. Stavros Coustakis still, it seemed, had a mind to be father-in-law to a Lakaris…

Well, he would not succeed! Anger bit into Xandros hard, aggravating his ill humour. There was one reason and one reason only why he'd come to London. And that was to confront this hitherto totally unheard-of daughter of Stavros Coustakis and disabuse her of any expectations that her father might have put into her head.

Marrying Ariadne, whom he'd known for years, would have been one thing—marrying her unknown English half-sister was an absurdity he wouldn't even give the time of day to! The very last thing he wanted was for the wretched girl to turn up in Athens and plague him!

Just remembering Stavros's unholy taunt to go and fetch his 'other daughter' made anger spear through him. But now there was a different cause for it. A completely different one he could scarcely bring himself to credit.

His laser gaze rested on the female standing frozen in front of him. He was still unable to believe she was who she said she was. Because it was impossible—just impossible!

Whoever Stavros's hitherto totally unknown other daughter was, she just could *not* be the woman standing here!

However brief the liaison Stavros might have had with the girl's mother, his child would have been amply provided for. Stavros Coustakis was one of the richest men in Greece! So his daughter would obviously be the London equivalent of Ariadne, living somewhere appropriate for having so wealthy a father! Somewhere like Chelsea or Notting Hill or Hampstead—

But the contact address that had been supplied to him by Stavros at his hotel a short while ago had made him frown. What would Stavros Coustakis's daughter be doing in this tatty, rundown part of London? Was she into property redevelopment, perhaps? Seeing financial opportunities in clearing semi-derelict sites and here merely to scope out potential projects?

The actual truth, forcing itself upon him now as he stared incredulously at the figure in front of him, was…unbelievable.

He felt shock resonate through him again now, and his gaze skewered her, taking in every dire detail of her appearance—the stained tee, the baggy cotton trousers covered in damp patches, the hands in yellow rubber gloves, clutching a floor mop and a bucket reeking of disinfectant. Her hair was screwed up on top of her head in a kind of topknot from which messy tufts protruded. And as for her face—

His expression changed. He'd been so negatively impacted by the grim first impression she'd made that it had been all that had registered. But now…

His eyes narrowed in automatic male assessment. Okay, so her complexion was pallid and blotchy, lined with fatigue, and there was a streak of dirt across her cheek, but other than that…

Fine-boned features, a tender mouth, and beautiful eyes that, despite the dark hollows beneath them, are—

Grey-green.

Shock ripped through him again. For all his protest that this appallingly attired, rubber-gloved female with her mop and bucket just could *not* be Stavros Coustakis's daughter, those eyes—so incredibly distinctive—proved his denial and disbelief wrong.

Thee mou—she really is his daughter.

Shock stabbed him again—and he saw the same emotion intensify in her frozen face as well.

'My *father*?' she gasped.

The mop clattered from Rosalie's suddenly nerveless grip. Her vision seemed to be blurring, the world turning fuzzy…

She had heard the man who had just spoken say what surely to God he could not have said…

Because I don't have a father. I've never had a father...never...

He was saying something in a foreign language. She didn't know what—didn't know anything except that the world was still turning fuzzy and she seemed to be falling…

Then, like iron, his grip seized upon her arm and she was bodily steered into the kitchen, forcibly propelled down on to the chair by the rickety table. At last the falling sensation stopped, and the world became less fuzzy, and she found herself blinking blankly.

The man was now standing in front of her, towering over her, and she was staring at him with that weird, blurry gaze. He was speaking again, and she forced herself to hear him.

'Your father—Stavros Coustakis,' he was saying.

She mouthed groggily. 'Stavros Cous… Cous…?' She tried to say the foreign-sounding name, but couldn't make her throat muscles work properly.

The man was frowning down at her, and with a part of her brain that should not have been working she registered how the frown angled the sculpted planes of his face, darkening those incredible dark eyes of his to make him even more ludicrously good-looking than ever, doing things to her that were utterly irrelevant right now, at this moment when he had told her what she had never expected to hear in all her life…

'Stavros Coustakis.'

She heard him repeat the name in the accented voice which went, she realised, with the foreign-sounding name he'd said—just as it went with the air of foreignness about him.

She blinked again, staring at him. 'I've got a father?'

The question sounded stupid, because he'd just told her she had, but she could see it had an effect on the man, because his frown deepened even more, drawing together his arched brows and furrowing his broad brow, deepening the lines scored around his mouth.

'You didn't know? You didn't know Stavros Coustakis was your father?'

There was incredulity in the man's voice, and Rosalie looked at him blankly. 'No,' she said.

The man seemed to be staring down at her as if not believing anything about her. Not believing she was who she'd told him she was. And not believing she didn't know this Stavros Cous-something-or-other was her father.

Her *father*…

The word rang in her head. A word she never used—for what would have been the point? It was a word that was utterly nothing to do with her, because he didn't exist—hadn't existed except for those pathetically few short weeks in her poor mother's life, when he had seemed to bring romance before departing for ever.

But suddenly now, at this very moment, he *did* exist.

She felt shock ricochet through her at the realisation, and it made her voice thready as she asked the question burning fiercely in her head. 'How did he find me?'

It came out in a rush, a blurting question, and she gazed hungrily at this man who had come here and dropped this amazing, incredible, unbelievable bombshell into her life—a life that had suddenly, out of no where, changed for ever.

My father knows about me! He's sent someone to find me!

Emotion leapt within her, distracting her from the fact that the dark eyes looking down at her had suddenly veiled.

'That is something you must ask him yourself,' was his clipped reply, but she leapt onwards to the next question.

'Where is he?' Her voice was avid, hungry, the words tumbling from her.

'He lives in Athens.'

'Athens?' Rosalie's eyes widened. Her father was *Greek*?

In her head her mother's voice echoed…

'He was foreign—so romantic!—working in London...'

'Yes.'

The man's voice was curt. She saw his face tighten, as if he were shutting her out of something.

'As for any other questions you may have, they can wait.' He glanced around himself. She could see his expression tighten even more. 'Get your things and we'll leave.'

Rosalie stared. 'What do you mean?'

That tight-lipped, angry look was back in his dark eyes.

'I'm taking you to Athens,' he said. 'To your father.'

Xandros glanced sideways at his passenger in the chauffeured car. She still had that blank expression on her face, as if she was not really taking in what was happening.

Make that two of us, Xandros thought grimly.

He'd come to London with no intention other than to warn Stavros's English daughter against her father's scheming. But now his anger at Stavros had found a new cause. Hell, he'd always known the man was ruthless—his disowning Ariadne was proof of that!—but what he'd done to this wretched other daughter of his was…unforgivable.

Keeping her in ignorance about her father—keeping her in abject poverty...

Emotion roiled in him, and there was a dark, angry glitter in his eyes. Stavros wanted his English daughter delivered to him in Athens? Well, Xandros would be glad to oblige! No way could he just walk away from her, leave her there in that slum…

She'd come eagerly enough—but then, why wouldn't

she? She'd just discovered she had a father she'd never known about—of *course* she'd want to meet him! And why delay? There was obviously nothing for her here in London! Not if she was reduced to cleaning for a living!

So he'd waited as she abandoned her bucket and mop, shed her yellow rubber gloves, shrugged on a cheap, worn jacket, picked up a shabby tote bag and left with him—just like that. She'd put the house key back through the letterbox and climbed into Xandros's waiting car.

She hadn't asked any more questions and Xandros had been glad of it. Answering them would have been difficult—especially any about how her father had found out about her existence.

His mouth set again. *Let Stavros tell her that to her face.*

There had been practical issues about getting her to Athens that had required immediate attention. Most importantly, did she have a passport? The answer had been an affirmative, and she'd told him it was in her bedsit. The car had stopped there—on another rundown street not far from the place she'd been cleaning—and Xandros's frown had deepened. The terraced house was peeling, its railings broken and rusty. Empty bottles and litter lay on the steps, and there were sagging curtains at the window. A total dump.

She hadn't taken long, emerging ten minutes later lugging a battered suitcase and climbing back into the car.

His eyes flicked over her now. She was looking marginally better, having changed into cheap faded jeans and a sweatshirt. Her hair was neater, and she had a strong odour of deodorant now—not stale sweat from a day's cleaning. Her skin was still pallid and blotchy, though, her features tired and drawn. Only her luminous grey-green eyes gave her beauty…

He snapped his gaze away, getting out his phone. What was it to him what Stavros Coustakis's English daughter looked like? His impulsive decision to take her to Athens had been motivated solely by his anger at the callous way Stavros had so obviously abandoned her to abject poverty.

Maybe Stavros will be shamed into supporting her now! Or she can hire a lawyer to make a claim—even take her story to the tabloids. How one of Greece's richest men left his own flesh and blood to live in squalor...

One thing that would *not* be happening, though, was Stavros's crazy idea that he might actually substitute this wretched, ill-treated English daughter—a total stranger to him!—for the missing Ariadne.

Xandros's mouth tightened. And if that meant he had to walk away from any hopes of the business merger he wanted—well, damnable though it would be to abandon a project he'd been determined on, so be it.

No way would he consider saving the merger by marrying Rosalie Jones…

He wouldn't give the thought the time of day.

CHAPTER TWO

ROSALIE SAT CLUTCHING her worn tote bag, staring out of the tinted window. She'd never been in a car with tinted windows—never been in a chauffeur-driven car. And she'd never sat next to a man like the one she was sitting next to now.

She pulled as far away from him as she could. He was checking messages on his phone now—a seriously flash model, she could see—and paying her no attention at all. She didn't care. She didn't want his attention anyway.

Alexandros Lakaris. That was what he'd said his name was. But who he was was not important. Nor was the fact that he was the most fabulous-looking male she'd ever seen in her life, let alone that she'd been looking a total mess when he'd first set eyes on her.

Those incredible, dark, long-lashed eyes had looked at her so disdainfully…

But why should she care what he thought of her? All that was important was what he'd told her.

She felt excitement rush through her again.

My father—he exists! He's real! And he's found out about me! He wants to meet me! My father!

The words were running through her head, storming through her like a torrent, overwhelming her, and she was only hanging on by a thread.

Everything was a daze.

In a daze she'd rushed up to her dive of a bedsit, grabbing what clothes she could, stuffing them into her suitcase. She'd riffled through the room for her passport—acquired so hopefully, yet never had there been an opportunity to use it—then hastily stripped off, washing in cold water at the tiny sink in the rickety kitchenette in the corner. Her hair was filthy, but there had been nothing she could do about that—nor the fact that she badly needed a shower. All she'd been able to do was spray herself with deodorant and put on clean clothes.

She hadn't impressed Alexandros Lakaris much, she thought now, with a twist of her mouth. She'd still got that disdainful flicker from his eyes when she'd clambered back into the car, depositing her battered suitcase in the footwell.

Oh, who cared what he thought of her? He didn't matter. Nothing mattered except the amazing, fantastic thing that was happening to her.

She felt a tearing at her heart.

Oh, Mum! If only you could have lived to see this—to see the man you fell for finding me! How wonderful that would have been!

The car was stopping and she frowned. They were going down Piccadilly, nearing Hyde Park Corner, and she'd assumed they were heading out towards the M4 and Heathrow. But they were pulling up outside a flash hotel.

Alexandros Lakaris was putting away his phone.

'What's happening?' she asked. 'Aren't we going to the airport?'

'The flight is tomorrow,' came the answer. 'I only arrived in London this morning. You'll stay at my hotel tonight.'

'I can't afford this place!' she exclaimed, horrified.

'But your father can,' Alexandros Lakaris informed her.

Rosalie saw his mouth tighten in a fashion that was becoming familiar. And his eyes were raking over her again in that disparaging way of his.

'He can also afford some new clothes for you before you fly out.'

She thought she saw a sudden unholy glitter in those incredible dark eyes she was so conscious of, try as she might not to be.

'You should go shopping,' he was saying, and there was a strange quality in his voice—a kind of smoothness that overlaid something quite jagged and pointed. 'There'll be time tomorrow morning before our flight.'

His eyes flickered over her, doing things to her they shouldn't but did all the same. Now they weren't disparaging. More like…assessing. She felt a sudden rush of ultra-self-consciousness that seemed to be heating her from the inside.

'And you might also want to take advantage of the facilities here at the hotel,' he went on in that same smooth voice. 'Hair salon, nail bar, beauty room—that sort of thing.'

Rosalie looked at him doubtfully. Surely that would be hideously expensive?

Alexandros Lakaris's expression had changed again. 'Charge it to the room,' he said now, as if seeing her reservations.

She swallowed. 'I don't want to cost my father too much,' she said.

That unholy glitter was there once more. As if something were amusing him. She didn't know what.

'Believe me…' his voice was as dry as desert sand '…he can afford it.'

Rosalie frowned. 'Are you sure?' she asked uncertainly. She could feel her stomach starting to churn. She pressed her hands together. 'Mr Lakaris, all I know about my father is what my mother told me—that he was foreign and was working on a construction site. A brickie—nothing more than that. So—'

He cut across her. 'Let's just say he's moved on since then. Now he has others to work for *him*.'

Her frown did not fade. Could what he was telling her be true? Belatedly she started to join up the dots she hadn't yet joined. Alexandros Lakaris—with his flash suit and gold tiepin, his polished handmade shoes and chauffeured car—was obviously a Mr Rich. And why would a Mr Rich have been sent as messenger boy to fetch her if not by another Mr Rich?

'How do you know my father?' she heard herself ask.

'We have a business association,' came his reply, said in an offhand fashion. 'I agreed to escort you to Athens for that reason.'

She opened her mouth to ask more questions, but he was opening his car door, getting out on his side. On her side a doorman came forward, opening her door and lifting out her suitcase as she stepped out on to the pavement.

Uncertainty still filled her—and confusion.

Could her father really afford all this? A hotel like

this…new clothes for her? But it must be true—or why would she be here?

A wash of excitement swept over her. Had her life really been transformed like this—out of nowhere and so amazingly?

The doorman was holding a huge plate glass door open for her and Rosalie went into the hotel, staring around her. It was very modern, with a soaring glass atrium and miles of marble floor.

Alexandros Lakaris was striding past her, walking in as if he owned the place, going up to one of an array of reception desks, obviously as at home in this five-star hotel as he'd been out of place in that rundown house she'd been cleaning.

This was his world—the world of expensive luxury…

She hurried after him, staring about her, clutching her tote and knowing how totally underdressed she was for such a plush hotel. Swish, elegant people were everywhere and her gaze swept over them. For a moment she quailed. Then she rallied, her chin going up.

I hate being poor—but I'm not ashamed of it! Why should I be?

But maybe…maybe all that was over now.

Maybe I'm done with poverty! Done with it for ever!

Her eyes lit with excitement, anticipation and a pleasure and thrill she had never known in all her impoverished life. She looked around the spectacular atrium, drinking it in.

Oh, boy, was she going to enjoy this!

'Your room key—you're on floor five.'

Alexandros Lakaris was holding out a piece of folded card that contained a plastic key pass. The frown that was becoming so familiar to her was back on his face.

Well, what did she care about his disapproval? He was nothing to her—just her father's messenger boy.

She kept her voice cool as she took her key. 'Thanks,' she said in a careless fashion. 'Let me know when I need to be ready tomorrow.'

She didn't wait for an answer—surely he could relay it to her through the hotel staff—and sauntered off towards the elevator banks.

Whatever Mr Oh-So-Handsome-and-Rich Lakaris, with his disapproving frown whenever he looked at her, was going to be doing till tomorrow, she couldn't care less. As for herself—she knew *exactly* what she was going to be doing.

She stepped inside a waiting elevator, and jabbed the number five, rolling her shoulders. They were stiff from her day's hard work. The overused muscles in her arms and legs were tired, and her hands felt like soggy sandpaper. The small of her back was aching, her knees knobbly from kneeling.

The elevator slowed, its doors slid open, and she stepped out into a lushly carpeted corridor, heading down towards her room on feet that were as tired and aching as the rest of her, but suddenly light as air.

Her drab and dreary life had been utterly transformed! Tomorrow she'd be flying to Athens—her first ever trip abroad!—to meet the father she had never known, who had now, like a miracle, discovered her existence! How fantastic was that? And for today—tonight—she was here in this amazing hotel and she was going to have a fabulous time, enjoying every last bit of what was happening to her!

Totally!

She couldn't wait…

* * *

Xandros checked his appearance in the en suite bathroom's mirror, minutely adjusting his bow tie. He was dressed for a formal dinner at one of the City's livery companies which he'd decided to attend that evening while he was here in London. It might prove a useful occasion to start what he would now, inevitably and annoyingly, have to undertake: prospecting for an alternative merger target.

His mouth thinned with displeasure and exasperation. His hopes for the Coustakis merger looked to be totally scuppered by his point-blank refusal to give the slightest attention to Stavros's outrageous scheming.

Did the man really think I would just swap from Ariadne to this other, totally unknown daughter?

It was ludicrously unrealistic—distasteful, even, for both himself and her—for Stavros to think that either of them would go along with it.

His thoughts strayed to the fifth floor…to Stavros's worn-down, shamefully neglected English daughter whom he'd so impulsively brought here. He knew what was behind that impulse—and it wasn't just his anger at Stavros. His face shadowed. Poverty was always frightening—even just the thought of it.

Memories from his own precarious childhood plucked at him. His parents, talking to each other in low voices, their expressions tense, talking about what further economies might next be made. His mother bewailing the fact that they might even lose the Lakaris family home. His father working long, punishing hours at the office, trying to salvage the wealth his own father had squandered.

The fact that he had done so—triumphantly—could

not take away the stress and uncertainty—and outright fear—that had dominated his youth and childhood even all these years later. So much so that the luxury he now enjoyed—and enjoy it he did—was appreciated to the hilt. It might so easily have been otherwise…

And hopefully now Stavros's English daughter, having known nothing but poverty all her life, condemned to cleaning filthy houses for a living, could look forward to an easier life, too.

He was glad he'd recommended that she do herself up, get some beauty treatments, buy some decent clothes, before she flew to Athens. After all, she was the daughter of one of the richest men in Greece—she should start looking as if she was!

What will she look like when she's dressed properly? Groomed properly?

He felt his masculine interest pique, a memory flickering of those hints of potential beauty behind her drab appearance, her luminous grey-green eyes. Her figure was good, even in the cheap jeans and sweatshirt…enticingly slender, yet full-breasted…

He snapped his thoughts away. They were inappropriate. He felt sorry for her—that was all. Nothing else.

He headed off for his dinner, resolutely putting her out of his mind.

Rosalie sighed luxuriously. This was bliss—bliss! And it had been ever since she'd slid the key card down the lock and stepped inside her hotel room.

What a room!

A vast bed, satin curtains, an armchair and a table, a massive wall-hung TV—and an en suite bathroom to die for! She'd tossed her bag down on the bed, kicked off her worn trainers and danced around in sheer glee. Then she'd sunk down on the huge soft bed and opened the leather brochure describing the hotel's facilities.

Moments later she'd been lifting the house phone… making a lengthy—a *very* lengthy—booking in the spa, to be cleansed and pampered to within an inch of her life! Wraps, facials, manicure, pedicure, haircut, massage… the lot!

Now, hours later, with all the fatigue and the aches and pains of her overworked body vanished, her skin like satin and her hair like silk, she was propped up against the pillows on her huge bed, idly surfing her way through the vast array of channels on the TV. She was replete from the gourmet meal delivered by Room Service, picking at delicious chocolates and polishing off a half-bottle of white wine from the minibar.

Heaven—just heaven!

To think that this morning I woke and had no idea at all I'd be ending the day like this!

And she'd be flying off tomorrow to meet the father she had never known…

Wonder and joy flooded through her—and then a twist of grief.

Oh, Mum—if only you could have lived to enjoy this, too! To know that the man you fell for so many years ago finally discovered us again...

She lifted her glass, emotions full within her. As she set it back on the bedside table a rap on the door sounded. She started, then realised it must be Room Service, back to collect the dinner trolley.

Levering herself off the bed, she padded to the door

in her complimentary bathrobe and slippers, opening it without thinking.

It wasn't Room Service. It was Alexandros Lakaris.

Xandros had been in two minds as to whether to check on Stavros's daughter on his return from his dinner or just leave her be. A reluctantly acknowledged sense of responsibility had led him to do the former. However much the girl was nothing to do with him, he'd plucked her out of her familiar surroundings and deposited her here, in what was obviously a totally alien environment for her. He'd better just make sure she was okay, and not doing anything stupid.

Like opening her hotel room door to anyone who knocked.

'You should have checked who it was before opening the door,' he reprimanded her.

For a second he thought he saw her eyes widen at seeing him. Then it was gone.

'I thought you were Room Service,' came the unconcerned answer. 'Anyway, what do you want?'

She sounded offhand, as if she couldn't care less.

'I wanted to make sure you were all right,' he replied evenly, keeping a tight rein on his annoyance at this indifference to his concern for her.

'I'm fine,' she answered. 'In fact—*blissful*!'

Her offhand manner vanished as she said the word, her face lighting in a smile for which there was only one word.

Radiant.

Xandros's breath caught. His eyes focussed sharply as he rcalised it was not just her smile that was making his breath catch. She had quite definitely undergone a whole bunch of beauty treatments…

The formerly pallid, blotchy skin was now clear and glowing, the lines of ingrained fatigue vanished, and there were no dark hollows underneath her distinctive grey-green eyes any more—eyes that were wide-set and luminous under finely arched brows. Her hair had obviously been washed, cut and styled, and was pinned up loosely, with delicate tendrils framing her face. She'd had a manicure, too. He could see the now smooth, long-fingered hand holding together the edges of her towelling robe, which was doing nothing to conceal the deep vee of smooth, pale flesh and the long line of her slender throat…

Without the slightest effort on his part, Xandros felt the start of a low, purring reaction stirring in him that came out of pure, unadulterated, raw masculine instinct.

Because there was something about talking at this late hour of the night to a woman standing in a hotel doorway wearing only a towelling robe and looking the way she was looking now. He had spent the evening dining well and drinking some very tolerable wines, with vintage port to follow, and something about the moment was really very…

Tempting.

Tempting, indeed…

The low purr intensified and he almost—*almost*—reached out his hand to draw a slow, exploring finger down that deep vee of her robe…almost let his other hand lift to her face, cup the delicate line of her jaw, tilt up her chin so that he could close in on her and lower his mouth to hers…to touch and taste those silken parted lips…

Thee mou! Am I insane?

He hauled his wayward thoughts away.

It's out of the question—totally out of the question!

Having anything to do with Stavros's English daughter other than the barest minimum was unthinkable.

'Good,' he said briskly, and continued in the same manner. 'I stopped by to tell you that we'll need to head for the airport after lunch. So you can have the morning for shopping. The concierge will book a personal shopper for you at one of the department stores to speed things up. Don't worry about how to pay. I'll cover it with the store directly for now and sort it with your father later.'

He would take a particular pleasure in sending a hefty bill to Stavros—and not just because the man owed his shamefully neglected daughter big-time. He was pretty damn sure that Stavros had known he'd be dismayed to see how unlike Ariadne his older daughter was. Ariadne—cultured and couture-clad—had been eminently suitable as a Lakaris bride…unlike her ill-dressed, downtrodden, impoverished London-born half-sister.

It would have amused Stavros, Xandros strongly suspected, envisaging Xandros's predicted discomfiture at the prospect of taking so unlikely a bride in order to achieve the merger he wanted.

His mouth tightened. Yes, well, not only had he no intention whatsoever of matrimony now—with either sister!—but he could also play games of his own. It would amuse *him* to deliver Rosalie Jones to Stavros looking the way the daughter of one of Greece's richest men *should* look. Deliver her—and walk away.

Because Stavros Coustakis was not going to game-play with him one single time more. He was done with it. *Done*.

He snapped his mind back to the present moment, keeping his voice and manner businesslike. 'When you've finished shopping I'll meet you in the hotel lobby and we'll head to the airport.' He gave her another brisk nod, keeping everything neutrally impersonal. 'So, until tomorrow, goodnight.'

He turned away, heading back to his own room.

Best not to think of Stavros Coustakis's English daughter.

However radiant her smile…

CHAPTER THREE

ROSALIE SANK INTO the hotel car that had been sent to collect her—and her treasure trove of purchases—from the very upmarket department store in Knightsbridge where she had just spent three fabulous hours in the hands of a personal shopper.

It had been heaven—a fantasy come to life!—to try on garment after garment, each and every one of them so incredibly beyond her normal clothes budget, which had been focussed all her life on the cheapest of chain stores and charity shops.

It had been beyond her wildest dreams. And it was all thanks to her father! The father she had never known—who had never known about *her*!

And now they were to meet—this very evening!

Excitement and happiness filled her to the core.

Back at the hotel, the myriad bags full of her purchases were whisked away to be packed into the new suitcases she'd also bought. Her battered old case, full of her battered old clothes, would be held in storage for the time being. It was all being taken care of.

Now all she had to do was have lunch in the hotel restaurant and be ready, as instructed, for departure for the airport at two thirty.

Her expression changed. Alexandros Lakaris had made it crystal clear that she was nothing more than a chore to him. It was just as well she'd resolved to treat him as nothing more than her father's messenger boy. Even if last night, when he'd turned up at her room door in that tailored tux of his, looking even more incredibly drop-dead fantastic than he had in a zillion-dollar business suit, she'd had to physically stop herself gawping at him and remember that he was nothing and nobody to her…

Well, it was obvious, wasn't it? She was equally nothing and nobody to him. So she would match his manner with hers—brisk and impersonal.

An hour later, with another heavenly gourmet meal inside her, she was enjoying to the hilt the knowledge that today, in one of her umpteen fabulous new outfits, unlike on her arrival yesterday, she looked exactly the part for a swish hotel like this.

She sailed out of the restaurant into the lobby.

Xandros glanced towards the entrance to the hotel restaurant where, so the reception clerk had informed him, Stavros's daughter was lunching. He had had a business lunch in the City, and now he wanted to head for the airport.

A woman was emerging from the restaurant, sashaying forward on high heels, her tall, elegant, long-legged figure cinched by a royal-blue waist-hugging fitted jacket with bracelet sleeves, and a narrow knee-length skirt. A pale blue silk chiffon scarf flowed behind her as she walked and her slender throat was adorned with a double rope of pale blue crystal beads. Long, lush blonde tresses waved back from her face…her perfectly made-up, beautiful face.

Stavros's daughter.

Rosalie Jones.

Shock jarred Xandros—the same level of shock he'd felt yesterday, when she'd announced her name to him, but for the totally opposite reason now.

Because now, as she sailed up to him, there was only one word to describe her.

Stunning. Just…*stunning.*

Unbelievably so.

His eyes raked over her, taking in every detail of her amazingly displayed beauty. Oh, he'd got hints of it last night, but now…in all her new finery, with her face perfectly made up, her hair fabulous, her figure fully revealed in that close-fitting outfit and her legs lengthened with those four-inch heels…now she was a revelation.

A stunning revelation.

Deep inside, he felt that same low, insistent purr that had come from nowhere last night when he'd seen her in her towelling robe. It was starting up in him again. Much more strongly… But this time, in the face of that incredible full-on beauty of hers, there was no chance of silencing it. Nor, he realised, did he want to. What he wanted was to enjoy the sheer, raw masculine pleasure of watching this totally stunning female walk up to him. Around her, he could see other male heads turning, and a primeval satisfaction filled him. Of all the men present in the hotel lobby, whether guest or staff, it was *him* whom she was heading towards…

It felt good. And he didn't care why.

She stopped in front of him. 'So, are we off?' she enquired briskly.

He gave a start, realising that he must stop just gazing fixedly at her.

'To the airport?' she prompted. She glanced towards the reception desk. 'I checked out before lunch,' she went on. 'The concierge has taken my old suitcase into storage. I'd better get the new ones,' she said.

She sashayed off to the concierge's desk, and Xandros paused for a moment to revel in the sight of her rear view. Her perfectly formed rear view...

He kept it in sight as they left the hotel and she got into the waiting car. Inside, as he took his place beside her, he let his gaze go to her face.

'So, you went shopping, I see?' he said, his voice dry. It would be sensible, he told himself, to stay low-key about this.

She turned towards him, and a waft of expensive perfume came his way as she did so. 'Oh, *yes*! It was *fabulous*!'

Just as it had the previous night, a showstopping smile lit up her face. And, just as it had last night, Xandros's breath caught.

'The personal shopper was brilliant—she knew exactly what would suit me and saved me a ton of time!' Rosalie Jones was enthusing.

Xandros allowed his glance to wash over her. It was enjoyable to let it do so. 'You look,' he said, 'very good.'

He felt a wash of pleasure go through him at the fact that he had ensured she had at least been able to indulge her a little after what had been, till now, a punishingly deprived life.

'I want to look my best for my father,' she was saying now, in answer to his compliment.

Her expression wavered for a moment, and there was a show of anxiety in it.

'I want him to be proud of me,' she said. 'To be pleased he's discovered I exist after all these years of not knowing. I only wish my poor mother had lived to see this day. How thrilled she'd have been!'

With an effort, dragging his attention away from her, taking in what she'd just said, Xandros kept his expression neutral. It was hard to hear her getting it so pitifully wrong about the callous and neglectful man who had fathered her. Hard to hear just how tough her life had been.

'Poor Mum!' she went on now, sadness in her voice. 'She only knew my father for such a short while and then he was gone. She couldn't trace him, so he never knew about me.'

She bit her lip again, her hands twisting over her brand-new elegant leather handbag.

'Knowing now that he's been successful in his life, it seems so dreadful that he didn't know about us before now. My mother's health was never good, and we had to survive on state benefits because she wasn't well enough to work, and I had to look after her… It was always a struggle. Always—'

She broke off, glancing at him.

'It meant I couldn't get a job either, or even any college education.' She gave a half-defiant shrug, 'That's why I have to do the work I'm doing. I'm living as cheaply as I can, saving as much money as I can. I've started evening classes…an online course—'

She broke off again, her expression changing.

'But now everything's changed! Now everything's going to be *wonderful*!'

The sadness had vanished from her voice and her face had brightened. She rested her gaze on Xandros, looking at him expectantly. Ruthlessly, he kept his own gaze inexpressive by sheer effort of will, though her sorry tale of all she'd been through had stung him.

I should tell her what Stavros is like! I should tell her not to push her hopes too high! Not to pin them on him at all!

But he could not bring himself to see her crash down so brutally.

And she's not my problem—not my concern!

That was what he had to remember. He slammed the stern instruction into himself. Just as he had to remember that, however amazing she looked—and he had not expected her to look anything like that—he should keep his instinctive male reaction to her firmly checked. It was at the very least...irrelevant.

I'm just taking her to Stavros—that's all.

And as for that—well, however much of a crushing disappointment Stavros Coustakis would turn out to be, even having a father like Stavros was better than the life she'd been leading up till now, wasn't it?

She'll get something from him, surely? Even if it takes lawyers or the tabloids to screw it out of him!

She was speaking again now, and he realised she'd asked a question. A question he didn't want to answer.

'So, how *did* he find out about me?'

Xandros's expression shuttered even more. 'Like I said yesterday, that's a discussion for you to have with him.'

To his relief, she only nodded, and moved on to another question.

'What else can you tell me about him? You said he's been successful in life, but in what way?'

'Construction, mostly,' Xandros answered, relieved the topic had moved on. 'But he's branched out since—insurance, financing…that kind of thing. He's a very shrewd businessman.'

'I'm glad for him,' she said. Then she paused, her expression changing, her manicured hands playing with the strap of her soft leather bag. She frowned. 'What about…well, his personal life? You see,' she went on in a rush, 'it's dawned on me that…that I might not be his only offspring!'

She lifted her eyes to Xandros—Stavros's distinctive grey-green eyes.

'Is he married?' she asked. There was a nervousness in her voice that he could actually hear.

He shook his head. 'He's widowed. His wife died some years ago. But…' He paused. 'But they had a daughter. A few years younger than you. Ariadne.'

He saw her eyes widen.

'Oh, that's wonderful! I have a sister! Oh, you don't know how wonderful that sounds! Will I meet her?'

Xandros shook his head again. 'She's abroad at the moment.' He tried not to sound evasive.

'Oh, that's a shame! I hope… I hope she won't mind having a sister…'

Xandros's expression tightened. Who knew what Ariadne would think about this unknown daughter of her father arriving out of nowhere?

'Do you know her? My sister?'

The artless question was unanswerable. Not without

explanations he had no intention of giving. So he only nodded, and to his relief realised his phone was ringing.

With a murmured 'Excuse me…' he answered it, grateful for the reprieve.

It was a reprieve he kept going till they arrived at Heathrow. Wading into the grim details of Stavros Coustakis's Machiavellian machinations was not something he was prepared to do.

He glanced sideways at the daughter Stavros had summoned to take the place of the daughter he'd disowned.

She'll cope with the situation when she discovers it—she'll have to!

And whether she would cope or not—whichever it was—it was not his problem and not his business. Because, for all his impulsive decision to take Rosalie Jones out to Greece to claim what she could of the heritage she'd been denied all her life, on one thing he remained adamant. Nothing—absolutely nothing—would induce him to fall in with her father's ludicrous plan for him to marry Ariadne's sister just to achieve the merger he was set on.

However stunningly beautiful she'd turned out to be…and however hard it was to drag his eyes from her…

Tiredness was lapping at Rosalie. Though it had been absolutely fantastic to enjoy her very first plane flight in first class, where champagne and a gourmet dinner had been served, and she'd loved nestling into her soft, capacious leather seat, flicking through complimentary high-fashion magazines as if to the manor born, the flight had been long and they'd landed in near darkness.

Greece, she'd discovered, was two hours ahead of the UK, and it would be nearly another hour before they arrived at her father's. He lived, so Alexandros Lakaris had informed her when she'd asked, in one of the most exclusive suburbs of Athens.

She couldn't wait to get there! To finally meet her father! But even all her excited anticipation couldn't stop her energy levels dropping away as they drove away from the airport. She felt flat, suddenly, and out of nowhere apprehensive.

'We're nearly there now.'

The voice at her side made her turn her head from peering out of the car window, though there wasn't much to be seen outside. It was so strange to think that she was in a foreign land.

But it isn't foreign! That's the whole point! It's the land of my father, and I'm as much Greek as I am British!

Yet as she made out the road signs in Greek lettering, and all the shopfronts, the traffic driving on the 'wrong' side of the road, it all seemed very alien.

The car was turning off the busy main road now, nosing down quieter roads that became spacious and tree-lined and less brightly lit by street lamps. At either side high walls girded the mansions hidden behind them, glimpsed only through steel gates. The car turned again, down yet another wide avenue, and then slowed in front of a pair of steel electronic gates. The driver spoke into a grille, and the gates swung open.

Rosalie felt her nerves tauten, her hands clutching at her handbag on her lap. The car moved slowly forward, over a crunching gravel carriage sweep, to pull up at the entrance to a white-fronted mansion, with wide steps leading up to huge double doors. The driver was getting out, opening her door.

She turned to the man who had brought her here, lifting her out of her grim, grinding, cheerless life in the East End of London to deposit her here at her father's house.

'Thank you for bringing me,' she said.

She made her voice bright, though she didn't feel bright. She felt nervous, but she wouldn't let it show.

Just like I didn't let it show that I could see, when I sailed out of the restaurant at the hotel, that he was finally changing his mind about me! That I finally wasn't invisible to him!

It had been a good moment, a gratifying one, and she had relished it. But it seemed a long time ago now.

Besides, what does it matter whether I'm invisible to him or not? Or that he's so incredible-looking? So what? It's my father I've come here for.

With a movement as graceful as she could make it, she got out of the car, gazing up at the imposing frontage of the house.

My father's home.

She tried to feel the excitement she should be feeling, but the nervous flatness that had come over her since landing was still paramount. She could hear the driver extracting the suitcases with all her expensive new clothes in them. The front door was opening—was this her father coming out to greet her? The father whom she had never known, who had never known about her...

But it was just a manservant in a white jacket, ushering her indoors with a murmur in Greek she didn't understand. Rosalie cast a look back at the car, where the driver was resuming his seat, and raised a brief hand in farewell to the man who had brought her here… Alexandros Lakaris.

Did he respond? The tinted windows made it impossible to know. And then the car was moving off around the carriage sweep, disappearing through the gates.

She turned and went inside her father's house.

She felt suddenly very alone.

Xandros sat back in his seat. For a moment, just before she'd walked up the steps, he'd had to suppress an impulse to get out and go in with her. Not to let that hapless girl face Stavros Coustakis all on her own.

He drew a breath. She wasn't his concern, and she certainly wasn't his responsibility. Rosalie Jones had entered his life briefly and now she had left it again. He would keep it that way and get back to his own life.

He lightened his expression determinedly. After Ariadne's rejection he'd felt a sense of freedom. He should heed it. He hadn't wanted to tie himself down—not in his heart of hearts—and now he wasn't going to.

As the car headed back into central Athens he let his mind play with pleasurable anticipation upon just how…and with whom!…he would celebrate this happy new freedom, enjoying the kind of affairs he was used to enjoying—the kind that never lasted and never led to anything longer than a few months.

His mind drifted over various females of his acquaintance, each of them a beauty, each of them, he knew from long experience, not averse to any sign of interest from him.

He felt an unwelcome frown form on his forehead, and his fingers started to tap impatiently on the armrest. There was one problem he was encountering in his mental parade of willing beauties. Not a single one of them held any allure for him whatsoever. And into his mind's eye was intruding one that did.

A showstopping figure, a cinched-in waist, endless legs, long, waving blonde hair...and grey-green eyes.

He slammed his thoughts shut. No—that was not going to happen…

Definitely, *definitely* not.

CHAPTER FOUR

ROSALIE LOOKED ABOUT HERSELF. It was a bedroom. She'd been shown up to it by the manservant, followed by two maids who'd started to unpack her suitcases until Rosalie had halted them. She was not comfortable with people waiting on her hand and foot.

She turned now to the manservant. 'When will I be seeing my father?' she asked in what she hoped was a casual fashion, hoping he spoke English.

He did, with a strong accent, but his words filled Rosalie with surprise and dismay.

'Kyrios Coustakis is out this evening,' he informed her in lofty tones. 'You will see him in the morning.'

She opened her mouth to speak, but now more maids were coming in, bringing in a dinner tray and coffee. The manservant bowed, and took his leave along with all the maids.

Rosalie stared at the door he'd shut behind him and felt a headache coming on. Tiredness snapped at her. Maybe, she thought, it was better that she postpone her all-important first encounter with her father till the morning, when she'd be fresher.

But the flatness that had assailed her since landing did not abate, even after she went to have a shower in what proved to be a highly opulent en suite bathroom, with gold taps and shower fittings and patterned marble on the walls.

Padding out into the bedroom, wrapped in a bath towel, she could see the room's opulence was just as lavish—there was gilding everywhere, from the bedframe and bedside table lamps to the gold-threaded drapes and massive chandelier.

The effect was… She puckered her brow. *Oppressive.*

With a sigh she sat herself down to pick at the food on an equally gilded tray. Lifting the silver dome revealed chicken in a very rich sauce, fried potatoes and beans. Though she felt bad about it, she couldn't face any of it, and soon replaced the dome, settling for just a bread roll and some strange-tasting butter. The coffee was strange, too—very thick, full of grounds, and there wasn't enough milk.

A wave of homesickness swept over her. Not for the festering bedsit she'd lived in till yesterday, but for the council flat where she'd grown up, where it had been just the two of them—she and her poor, frail, ill mum, all that each other had had, the two of them against the world, alone in the little flat. It had been small and shabby, and paying the bills and putting food on the table had always been a grim challenge, where every penny had done the work of two, but it had been *home…*

But this is home now. My father's home. My home.

The word hung strangely in the centre of her consciousness. Home? Was that what this huge, over-opulent, servant-staffed house was to be for her now?

She felt a heavy sigh escape her. One that should not

have. For surely coming here, to her father, would be the best thing that had ever happened to her?

As she went to climb into the huge too-soft bed, with its satin sheets that were too slippery, she made herself imagine their meeting tomorrow. Made it vivid in her mind.

He'll sweep me into his arms! Hug me close! Tears in his eyes and mine! And it will be wonderful! Oh, so wonderful!

As sleep closed over her she wanted to dream of it—dream of the magical meeting that awaited her. But the dreams that came were not of her unknown father. They were of the man he'd sent to fetch her. Who meant nothing to her—nothing at all.

He was only a handsome stranger who had delivered her here and then driven off again into the night, job done. Disposing of her like an unwanted parcel.

No one worth dreaming about.

'Kyrios Coustakis will see you now.'

The stately manservant was standing at Rosalie's open bedroom door. She turned from the window. Strong sunlight was shafting across what the morning light showed to be a manicured garden, with fountains, gravelled paths and close-clipped topiary. A garden that looked impressive from the house.

But she wasn't here to think about ornamental gardens. She was here to go downstairs and finally meet the man who, over a quarter of a century ago, had encountered her mother and brought her into existence.

Emotion knifed in her, but she controlled it. So much was welling up in her, but she dared not let it out. Yet.

Her heart was thumping as she followed the manservant downstairs. She'd dressed with extreme care, wanting to give her father no cause for disappointment or disapproval. Her smart yellow shift dress was knee-length, with cap sleeves and a round neckline, her hair was drawn back into a neat chignon, and she wore minimal make up. Her heels were low, and they clicked as she went down the sweeping marble stairs and across the imposing entrance hallway.

The manservant knocked discreetly at a pair of double doors set opposite, and Rosalie heard a voice say sharply in Greek, what she supposed was 'Enter' or 'Come in.'

The manservant opened the door and Rosalie walked in. Her heart was thumping like a jackhammer with anticipation. With hope.

The man who must be her father was seated at a desk across an expanse of tapestried carpet, and the whole room was lined with floor-to-ceiling bookcases filled with books. It was at once impressive and intimidating, Rosalie registered, with the part of her brain that was not focussed on the man watching her approach.

But her eyes were only for her father—fixed on him. She reached the desk, expecting him to stand up, come to greet her. Embrace her. Welcome her to his life.

But he did not. He simply sat back in his chair. Looking her over.

'So,' he announced, 'you are here.'

His gaze was like a gimlet and then he made a sudden gesture with his hand. 'Turn around.'

Rosalie stared, eyes widening. Suddenly it was as if there was sand in her throat. Why wasn't he getting up and coming to her, greeting her, hugging her?

'I said turn around.'

Her father's voice, strongly accented, had sharpened, as though he disliked not being obeyed immediately.

A frown creased Rosalie's brow. 'What for?' She heard the words come from her without her volition, in an automatic response to an order.

Something snapped in his eyes. 'Because I tell you to!'

'You *tell* me to?' There was disbelief in her voice.

She saw his eyes snap again.

Grey-green eyes, like mine.

The thought flitted across her brain, but she had no time for it. He was speaking again.

'If you want what I can give you, you will do what I tell you!' Something changed in his voice—something that made it not sharp, but as if something were twisting it out of true. 'And I can see from your expensive get-up that you *do*, indeed, want what I can give you. *If* I choose to do so!'

He sat back in his chair, steepling his fingers.

'Do you understand the situation now?'

Rosalie shook her head. No, she did not understand the situation. She did not understand it at all. This was her *father*. And yet he was speaking to her as if she were a…a servant! A lowly employee… Not as his long-lost daughter at all…

She felt something stab inside her—a pain so sharp that she felt it pierce to her core. But she also felt the force of what he'd just said. She'd rushed out to buy designer clothes the moment she knew she could.

'I…I'm sorry…' The words stumbled from her. 'I…I bought nice clothes because I thought…thought you would like me to look…nice…for you. I wanted to please you—' She could hear her voice catch as she spoke, but couldn't prevent it. 'I didn't mean to waste your money!' she finished in a rush of apology.

Her father's expression changed. Sharpened almost to the point of glinting.

'You won't—be assured of that,' he retorted. 'And if you wish to please me do as I tell you. Turn around!'

Tautly, Rosalie did what he bade. As she came full circle he was nodding, his expression less sharp.

'That's better,' he informed her. His gimlet eyes rested on her face assessingly, his hands still steepled. 'You have my eyes—good. The rest must come from your mother. I remember very little about her.'

'She remembered you!' Rosalie cried out before she could stop herself. 'She told me everything she could—'

Her father's expression changed again. There was a cynical light in his eyes now. 'I made sure there wasn't much to know. And I kept it that way.'

A frown furrowed Rosalie's brow. She could feel her emotions tightening within her, still feel that pain inside—because this wasn't right… This wasn't right at all. This wasn't the way it was supposed to be…

'So…so how did you find out about me? My mother told me that she tried to get in touch when she learnt she was pregnant, by writing to the construction company, but you must have left the country already because she never heard back. Her letter must never have reached you—'

'Of *course* it reached me!'

A gasp broke from Rosalie and she stared at the man across the desk from her.

An impatient look crossed his face. 'I've always known of your existence.'

Rosalie stared on. Inside her, a stone seemed to be occupying her entire lung capacity.

'You've *always known*?' The words forced themselves past the stone that was choking her.

'Of course!'

'You've *known* and never got in touch?'

'Why should I have?'

'*Why?* Because I am your *daughter*!'

A sneer had formed on his face—Rosalie could see it. Was appalled by it. Appalled by everything that was happening…

'What was that to *me*?' he retorted. 'Nothing! What possible interest could I have had in you, or your fool of a mother?' His face tightened, an expression of angry displeasure forming. 'You have been of no use to me until now. Which is why I sent for you.'

Emotion was storming in Rosalie, hard and angry and desperately painful.

'You knew about me and did *nothing*? Nothing to *help*? Did you *know* how ill my mother was?'

The grey-green eyes so hideously like her own flashed again.

'She was a fool, like I said! A clinging, feeble-minded fool! As for you—the state looked after you as a child… Your mother got child support, a flat to live in. Why would I waste *my* money on you?'

The harsh, cruel words about her hapless mother struck her like blows and she flinched to hear them. Protest rose in her, and she sent an arm flying out to encompass the opulence of the room she stood in, the grandeur of this mansion her father lived in.

'You're *rich*! We were so poor—grindingly poor!

Mum was so ill she couldn't work, and I couldn't either because I had to look after her—'

A hand slammed down on the desk's tooled surface with heavy force. 'Be silent! Don't come crying to me! My money is *mine*—do you understand? Mine to do with *exactly* as I like!' His face hardened. 'And if you want to enjoy a single cent of it you'll change your attitude, my girl!'

Rosalie's face froze. She'd heard the last of his outburst—*'my girl!'*—and it was as if the words were acid on her skin.

But I'm not his girl—I'm no more his daughter than a block of wood! He knew... He knew about me and never cared at all...

The words tumbled through her stricken brain like spiked wheels, each one inflicting stab after stab of pain.

As if through a mist she saw her father get to his feet, come around the desk. For a moment, a wild, last frantic flare of the pitiful emotion that had been filling her ever since Alexandros Lakaris had made that astounding announcement leapt within her as for the briefest space of time she thought he was coming to her now, to embrace her in a crushing, paternal, loving embrace…

Her father, after all these long, empty years…

But he simply reached out to take her elbow and steer her bodily towards a pair of ornate chairs a little way from the desk.

'Sit,' he instructed, and lowered himself heavily on to the other chair.

Like a dummy, she did so, her legs suddenly weak.

He nodded. 'Now that you have divested yourself

of whatever sentimental rubbish was in your head, you can listen to me.'

His eyes rested on her like heavy weights. They were puffy eyes, she found herself registering abstractedly, irrelevantly, and there were deep lines scored around his mouth, which was thin and tightly set.

'You need not think that you won't come out of this a great deal better off than you have been all your life,' he continued, and there was less harshness in his voice now, as if he were adapting it to what he was saying. 'On the contrary. This is your lucky day indeed, I promise you! You will be able to live up to the clothes you have so eagerly rushed out to acquire! You'll be able to buy ten times that number! Live a life of idle luxury! Buy anything you want! Have anything you want!'

His voice altered again, the expression in his eyes changing, and Rosalie sat there numbed, yet with her mind filled with knives, her lungs choked.

'Tell me,' she heard him say, as if from far, far away, as if she weren't really sitting there, unable to move, filled with horror and disbelief at the ugly truth of the dream she had so stupidly woven in her head, 'what did you make of our handsome Alexandros, eh?'

She stared…swallowed. 'Alexandros Lakaris?' she echoed, as if she had not heard aright. Why was this man who was her father but not her father—no, never her father—saying the name of the man he had sent to bring her here?

'Yes, the handsome and oh, so well-born Alexandros Lakaris! So eager to go and find you and bring you to Athens!'

There was a twist in his voice, and Rosalie could hear amusement—a cruel amusement.

'So eager to do what is necessary to achieve what he wants. Tell me,' he said again, and the thin mouth twisted, and there was a glint in the grey-green eyes as if he took pleasure in what he was saying, 'just how disappointed *was* he when he found you? My daughter—charring for a living! Hah! How that must have galled him!'

His thin mouth set. 'So, was it he who had you cleaned up and dressed to come here?' A harsh laugh broke from him and his hands clenched the arms of his chair. 'Not that it would have mattered a jot to *him*! It's just a bonus that you've turned out to be a looker, despite your origins, if enough money is spent on you! He can thank his lucky stars for that—and so can you! You'll enjoy your luxury lifestyle *and* Alexandros Lakaris as well! Every woman in Athens will envy you!'

The grey-green eyes sparked again, with gratified relish.

'And I will get exactly what I want, as I always do! A lordly Lakaris for a son-in-law!'

Rosalie stared at him, as if from a long, long way away.

'Son-in-law?' The syllables dropped from her mouth uncomprehendingly.

She saw the man who was her father and yet would never, *never* be her father lift his hand in a swift, impatient gesture.

'Of *course* my son-in-law! Why else do you imagine I have had you brought here? To marry Alexandros Lakaris, of course!'

She heard him say it, and yet did not hear him. Her mind was reeling, as if she were in a car crash that was going on and on and on, and she could not get out of it, could not escape it…

'You're mad…'

The blunt words were hollow as she spoke them. And she saw the face of the man who'd just told her the most impossible, insane thing in the world—the man who had only moments earlier smashed to pieces the idiocy she'd conjured up in her stupid, *stupid* brain—twist with anger at her retort.

'Do *not* try my patience! It is all arranged—all agreed. Alexandros Lakaris wants to merge his business with mine, and it is an excellent financial prospect for both of us. But I will only let him do so for a price. The price is you. *Thee mou*, what is there for you to look like that for? You've seen the man! I tell you again, every woman in Athens will envy you!'

'You're mad…' She said the words again, but this time, finding some last vestige of strength in her boneless limbs, she forced herself to her feet. She was in a nightmare—a living nightmare.

She turned away, wanting only to get out of there—get out of the room, get out…

Her father's harsh, ugly voice slashed through the air.

'Walk away from me now and you walk away completely! You can go back to the slums of London! Back to the gutter! You will get nothing—*nothing* from me!'

She turned. Her face was like stone. 'Go to hell!' she said.

And she left the room, tears and misery choking her throat at the ruination of all her dreams.

Xandros sat at his desk, unable to concentrate on what he should be doing—going about the daily routine of his business life. Instead an image was playing in his head. Tugging at his conscience…

The way he'd just driven off last night as Stavros's unwitting daughter had been swallowed up into her father's oppressive mansion... Walking in there with all her dreams about some fairy-tale reunion with a father who would embrace her lovingly and welcome her into his life.

His mouth set. Well, she'd have been disabused of *that* by now. Presumably they'd met, and she'd realised just what kind of a man Stavros was.

She'll be devastated...

The words were in his head and he could not stop them. Nor could he stop himself suddenly pushing back his chair and getting to his feet. He flicked the intercom and told his secretary he was heading out for a while, that she should cancel his scheduled meeting with his finance director.

Reluctance warred with his conscience. No, he did *not* want to have anything more to do with that toxic set-up, and, no, Stavros Coustakis's English daughter was *not* his concern, let alone his responsibility, but for all that...

I can't just abandon her like that.

That was the brute truth of it. Like it or not, he should have given her some warning of what to expect, and not let her indulge herself in illusions of some kind of heavenly reunion. He should at least check that she was...well, *coping* with the situation.

Ten minutes later he was in his car and heading out of central Athens. His plan was vague, but it focussed on calling at the Coustakis mansion...enquiring after the girl. Just checking that she was okay...salving his conscience.

And most definitely he would not let his eyes rest

once more on the astonishingly revealed beauty that had so unexpectedly emerged from behind that wretched bucket and mop image of his first sight of her. He crushed the thought instantly, before it could take any shape at all.

No, that was *not* the reason he was checking up on Rosalie Jones. Not at all…

Rosalie was walking. Rapidly, blindly and with one purpose only: to find some kind of public transport—a bus, a tram, a train…she didn't care what—to get her to the airport. Where she would raid her meagre savings to buy the cheapest possible ticket back to the UK.

Because anything else was impossible. Just impossible!

Emotions knifed in her, anger and misery, both of them stabbing and slicing away at her. Hot tears stung her eyes as she hurried, head down, clutching the handbag that held her precious passport and wallet. She was oblivious to everything except her need to reach the main road. Oblivious to the low, lean car suddenly pulling up beside her at the kerb.

She saw it only when a figure suddenly vaulted in front of her, tall and blocking out the morning sunshine. She stopped dead, her head jerking up.

Alexandros Lakaris was striding towards her, catching her arm.

'What's happened?'

His voice was sharp and she stared blindly at him, the hot, stinging tears in her eyes making him misty. She saw him frown, heard him say something in Greek just as sharp.

'I'm going back to England!' she bit out. 'I need to get to the airport! There has to be a bus, or a tram, or—'

He cut across her. His expression was grim. 'We need to talk,' he said.

Violently she yanked her arm free. 'No, we do *not* need to talk! I've *had* my talk! And my *father*—' she said the word with a twist in her voice that was like swallowing acid '—has explained *everything* to me! So, Mr Alexandros Lakaris, we do *not* need to talk! I am having *nothing* to do with my father's total *insanity*! And nothing to do with *him*!'

She heard Alexandros Lakaris take a harshly incised breath. Alexandros Lakaris—the man who, so her monstrous father had just informed her, had brought her to Athens solely and specifically for the purpose of marrying her, so he could do some kind of lucrative business deal with the foul, despicable man who had said such cruel things about her poor mother, who had treated her so callously—the vile pig of a man who she was now ashamed to call her father.

'Just what has he said to you?' Alexandros Lakaris bit out, his face dark, his eyes darker. He took another heavy breath, his mouth tightening, shaking his head. 'I should have warned you—prepared you—'

Words burst from Rosalie, exploding from her. 'He said he's always known about me! He's known about me from the very start! He's known about me and he has done nothing! Nothing at all! He left my poor, poor mother to cope all on her own! He didn't lift a finger! Just left us to *rot*!'

Her voice was broken, choking on what she was saying, facing up to. It was as if she couldn't stop the words pouring from her—couldn't stop the hot, stinging tears streaming down her face.

'He let her live on child benefit, grateful for a council flat! He *let* her and he didn't care! Not even when he got rich! He could have sent money, made some maintenance payments for me—he could have *helped* her!' The sobs were tearing from her now, and her voice was choking and broken. 'He has so *much* and we had *nothing*! But he didn't care—he just didn't *care*!'

She couldn't say any more. Her face was convulsing, her shoulders shaking with emotion. All those years of struggling and making do, of her poor, sick mother coughing up her lungs in their damp flat, eking out every last penny, dreading every bill that arrived until finally the end had come and she had died in poverty and bleakness. And she herself, homeless after the flat had been repossessed by the council, reduced to living in that stinking dive of a bedsit, working every hour of the day cleaning up other people's filth, studying into the small hours of the night to get the qualifications she'd need to lift herself out of the grinding poverty she'd lived in all her life.

And her father had known and done nothing—*nothing*—to lift a finger to help either of them!

It burned in her like acid and she could not bear it—she just could not bear it.

She was shaking like a leaf, choking and trembling, sobbing out hot tears…

CHAPTER FIVE

AND THEN ARMS were coming around her. Arms that were holding her, cradling her, letting her sob and sob for all the sadness and bleakness of her mother's life, of her own…sob for the cruelty and callousness of the man she had to call her father when she would have torn every shred of his DNA from her body if she could.

She sobbed until there were no more tears in her, barely conscious of the hard chest she was collapsed against, of the strong arms around her, holding her. The same hands that were now carefully, slowly, setting her back on her feet as her anguished sobs died finally away. A handkerchief was being handed to her, fine cotton and huge, and she took it, blowing her nose and wiping away the remnants of her tears, blinking to clear her blurred vision.

Alexandros Lakaris was speaking, and his voice held something she'd never heard in it before. It was the last thing she'd expected from him after the impersonal brusqueness he'd treated her with in London.

Kindness.

'Come, let me give you a lift—it's the least I can do.'

He ushered her towards the car and she sank down into the low leather seat, her legs weak suddenly, her whole body exhausted. She was drained of all emotion. Barely aware of what was happening.

He got into the driver's seat, pulled her seat belt across and fastened it. Then he turned to her. When he spoke the kindness was there in his voice again, but now she could also hear apology.

'I'm sorry,' he said. 'Sorry that I didn't warn you. Sorry that I just left you there last night.' He took a heavy breath. 'I'm sorry that you had to find out just what sort of man your father is.'

She saw his expression alter, his face set. Absently, with a part of her brain that was working even though it shouldn't be, because it was quite irrelevant, she was aware all over again of just how incredibly good-looking he was, with his deep-set, long-lashed, dark, dark eyes and his sculpted mouth, and his chiselled jawline and sable hair.

Unwillingly, in her head, she heard her father's hateful words score into her. *'Every woman in Athens will envy you—'*

She tore them from her. Tore away everything else he'd said. Every outrageous, appalling word…

How could he even think it—let alone assume it?

But she wouldn't think about what he'd said. Wouldn't give it the time of day.

The man sitting beside her—the man her despicable, monstrous father had said such things about—was speaking again, his voice sombre and heavy.

'Stavros Coustakis is not known for caring about other people,' he said tersely. 'But he *is* known for manipulating people for his own ends.'

Rosalie felt his gaze on her, as if he was assessing

how she was going to take what he was telling her. She stilled. Heard him go on.

'That's what he's been trying to do with me—and...' He paused, his dark eyes now holding hers quite deliberately. 'It's what he's tried to do with you.'

His mouth thinned again, and he drummed his fingers on the dashboard.

'Look, like it or not, we do need to talk. There are things I need to explain to you. Things you need to know. But not in this cramped car.' He suddenly gunned the engine, which made a low, throaty noise. 'I'll take you to lunch.' He held up a hand, as if she were going to protest. 'Then afterwards I'll get you to the airport, okay?'

Rosalie's face worked. He was being different, somehow. It was as if he were speaking to her for the first time. Speaking honestly—not concealing anything. And that, she realised slowly, was why he'd been so brusque with her in London.

Because he knew all along what I'd be facing when I met my father.

Well, now she knew, too—and it had devastated her. Repulsed her.

She nodded numbly. 'Okay,' she said, her voice low. She was not able to summon the energy to say anything else.

In her lap she twisted his handkerchief, then busied herself stuffing it into her handbag. He would hardly want it now, all soggy and used.

She sat back, exhausted suddenly. It had all been too much. Much too much. Too much for anything except sitting here, staring out of the window, saying nothing, letting Alexandros Lakaris drive her wherever it was he was taking her.

Where it was was the seaside.

She surfaced from the numbness in her head sometime later, and stared through the windscreen at the expanse of bright blue sunlit sea appearing as they reached the coast.

'Welcome to the Aegean,' said Alexandros Lakaris.

He pulled up outside a swish-looking restaurant on the seafront, flanking an even swisher-looking marina, where swisher yet yachts bobbed at their moorings.

He got out, and Rosalie found herself doing likewise—found herself breathing in the warm, fresh, salty air, lifting her face to the bright sunshine as it shone down on that blue, blue sea. Out of nowhere she felt the oppression and misery encompassing her lift a fraction.

She looked about her. There was a promenade opposite the restaurant and people were sauntering along. There was a pebbly, shingly beach beyond, and an air of leisure and relaxation.

'This is where Athenians come to get out of the city,' Alexandros Lakaris was saying.

'It's lovely,' Rosalie heard herself reply, and she heard her voice warming, in spite of all the misery still locked inside her.

'It's not the best the Aegean has to offer, but it's good for somewhere so close to Athens. Anyway, let's get some lunch.'

He steered her into the restaurant, which wasn't too busy, and they were soon seated at a table that was indoors, but open to the pavement seating area of the restaurant. Menus were set in front of them, and with a start Rosalie realised she was hungry.

After the emotions of the morning it seemed like a balm to her to be doing something so simple as sitting here, ordering lunch. Even though she still seemed to be drained dry, incapable of thought or decision.

I'll just go with what's happening at the moment. I can't do anything else—not now.

The food appeared swiftly. They'd both ordered fish, and it was served grilled, with rice and fresh salad, and it was, Rosalie discovered, extremely tasty.

Alexandros Lakaris didn't make conversation, just let her eat in silence. But it was a silence she could cope with, even welcome. The warm breeze off the sea caught at the tablecloth, fluttered the flags on the yachts, and the sun was still dancing off the little waves on the sea. It was calm, peaceful, and she was grateful for it. Glad of it.

She pushed her empty plate away. Her misery felt less now.

'Better?' Alexandros Lakaris asked.

She nodded. He was still being different from the way he'd been with her in London. It was as if something were changing between them, though she didn't quite know what. He beckoned to the waiter to remove their plates, ordered coffee, looked back at Rosalie.

'Then I think it's time we talked,' he said.

Xandros sat back, his eyes resting on the face of Stavros Coustakis's daughter, who had just had had her hopeless dreams about her father ripped from her and the ugly truth shoved in her face. He gave an inward sigh, compunction smiting him. Yes, he should have warned her—but he hadn't, and now he must make up for that omission.

She was looking a little better than she had when he'd found her storming away from the Coustakis mansion—that, at least, was something.

He felt emotion pluck at him. Taking her into his arms as she'd sobbed out her rage and misery had been an instinctive gesture. But it had felt good to hold her in his arms…good to feel her soft, slender body folded against his. Good to let his gaze rest on her.

Okay, any make-up she might have been wearing had been washed off in her flood of understandable tears, but her beauty was undimmed for all that.

He felt thoughts flickering somewhere deep in his brain—thoughts he shouldn't grant admittance, but which went on flickering all the same.

He did his best to ignore them.

'Whatever your father may have told you, this is what you need to know,' he began.

He reached for his coffee, took a large mouthful, needing the caffeine. He would keep this as simple as possible.

'The reason I am involved with your father is that I am keen to pursue a business merger with him. Not the construction side—that isn't my thing—but in his investment- and finance-based operations. They would fit perfectly with my own business enterprises and add considerable value to both of us. Your father knows that as well as I do. However—' he took a breath '—your father is also entertaining other ideas. He wants more than a mere business merger.'

He eyed Rosalie carefully. Her expression had been changing as he'd spoken—and not for the better.

'He wants,' he said, 'to merge our families.'

There—he'd said it. And it was like setting a match to dry tinder.

The grey-green eyes—her undeniable heritage from Stavros—flashed like knives.

'He *informed* me—' she bit out every word '—that *apparently* every woman in Athens would envy me when I became your wife.'

The deep, vicious sarcasm in her voice was coruscating.

Beneath his breath Xandros cursed fluently and expressively.

Stavros's daughter ploughed on. 'And he told me that if I did *not* choose to arouse that envy in the breast of every woman in Athens I could take myself back to my London slum and I would never see a single cent of his precious bloody money!'

He saw her jaw set like iron, her eyes stony.

'Which is exactly what I am doing,' she finished bleakly. 'I wish to God you had never found me!' There was a tearing sound in her voice now. Her features twisted. 'Why didn't you *tell* me that was the only reason you'd trekked to London? To bring me here so you and he could cook up some *insane* way to seal a business deal?'

There was incredulity in her voice, as well as anger.

'It wasn't like that,' Xandros said, his voice tight. 'Your father wanted that, but I…' he took a heavy in-breath '…I never had the slightest intention of doing what Stavros wanted! My sole aim in going to London at his bidding was to make it clear to you that whatever your father might have told you about his ambitions for a marriage-based merger I, for one, would not be cooperating!'

He paused again, and then went on. He had to say this next bit…

'As for why I ended up bringing you out here after all,' he went on, hardening his voice automatically, 'bear in mind that I'd naturally assumed that, as Stavros's daughter, you would be living the kind of affluent life similar to your sister's here in Athens.' His expression darkened. 'Once I'd seen—to my absolute shock and disbelief—that the daughter of one of Greece's richest men was living in the kind of poverty she should never have had to endure, how could I leave you there?'

He took another breath.

'So I resolved to bring you to Athens,' he went on. 'In the hope that once you knew the truth about your father, just how rich he is, you might…well…' he gave a shrug '…if not shame him into providing for you, at least you get *something* out of the brutal fact that Stavros Coustakis is your biological father! As for the merger… *All* I want is a business merger. Believe me!' he finished feelingly.

He glanced away, out over the promenade to the sea beyond, then looked back at her again. He had to say the rest of this now. She deserved as much.

'The reason your father wanted you brought from London,' he said, 'was because your half-sister also refused to go along with his scheme.'

He saw her eyes widen in shock.

'He wanted you to marry *Ariadne*?'

He nodded. He would keep this as brief as possible. 'She refused. Left the country.' He watched her expression change. Become bitter.

'So, after ignoring my existence all my life, he found

I was suddenly useful to him…' Her voice was hollow, and the bleakness was back in it.

Xandros reached for his coffee, which he needed now more than ever. 'That's about it,' he agreed tightly.

He found himself thinking that Stavros would have assumed that, unlike Ariadne, who had her mother's family to turn to, this East End daughter he'd knowingly and deliberately kept poor would be open to both his bribery and his threats.

Well, Rosalie Jones had rejected both all the same. She was, or so it seemed, prepared to return to her grim, impoverished life rather than be subject to her father's machinations in exchange for a life of ease. He felt admiration for her resolve fill him. Yet he knew it was a resolve that would cost her dearly.

He set his drained coffee cup back on the table. 'Are you really set on going back to London?' he asked.

She nodded, her mouth set, her expression bleak at the prospect—and who could blame her?

The image of how he'd found her, looking exhausted and worn down, reeking of bleach and worse, that mop and bucket in her rubber-gloved hands, was suddenly and vividly—unacceptably—in his head.

I can't let her go back to that!

'No.'

The word fell from his lips, instinctive and automatic. Adamant. A frown flashed across his face. No, she would *not* go back to that appalling, poverty-stricken life! It was unthinkable—unthinkable for the daughter of one of Greece's richest men! Surely he could help her get *some* degree of recompense from her father—find her a lawyer ready to take up her cause? Or a tabloid journalist? Or both?

Her outburst cut across his cogitations.

'I don't have a *choice*!' she threw back at him, her voice bitter. 'I refuse to have *anything* to do with a man who has said such vile, cruel things about my poor mother! Who knew he'd got her pregnant and then deserted her anyway, condemning her to a misery she endured for the rest of her tormented life without lifting a finger to help her—let alone the daughter he knew perfectly well he had! He can rot in hell for that! And for thinking he could *buy* me with his bloody money and that I'd *crawl* to him for it so I wouldn't have to go back to the poverty he deliberately kept me in, hoping it would make me malleable and desperate!'

Xandros could see her face working again, could hear the rage in her voice mounting once more. The fire in her eyes was making them more luminous than ever… her fury was animating her features…intensifying her beauty…

From somewhere deep in that part of his brain he'd had to silence before, the part that he had refused to pay any attention to, came a thought that was so outrageous he tried to stifle it at birth.

But it would not be stifled. Would not be silenced.

Because there was another way she could avoid being condemned to a life of grinding poverty. His mind raced. A way that would simultaneously do *him* some good as well. A considerable amount of good.

As his eyes rested on her agitated, stricken face, which for all the emotion working in it was still not diminished in its effect, on the emotion flashing in her eyes, lighting them into a blaze, he heard words rise up in his throat. Insane, surely, as it would be to say them…

And then he said them anyway.

'What if there was a different alternative?'

His eyes held hers, holding them by the sheer power of the will that was welling up in him from that deep, impossible place in his brain.

She stared. Blankness was in her face.

'What alternative?'

He held her eyes still—those beautiful, expressive eyes of hers—masking his own expression. But beneath the mask his thoughts were churning wildly. Was he really going to say what he was about to say? Could he mean it?

Then there was no more time for questioning himself, for he could hear himself speak. Saying the words.

'You marry me after all.'

She was staring at him. The blankness on her face was gone. And her expression now was one of total rejection.

'Hear me out,' Xandros urged. He was marshalling his own thoughts, moving them rapidly across his consciousness as they formed. 'You marry me—just as your father wants,' he repeated. *'But—'* and the emphasis was absolute '—you do so on *your* terms—not his.'

Her grey-green eyes were still stony with repudiation so he went on, hearing his own thoughts springing into being.

This will work! And it will work infinitely better than the marriage I was prepared to undertake with Ariadne! Because what made me so reluctant about Ariadne was the prospect of a permanent marriage! Of tying myself to her...having children! Losing my freedom.

But the marriage that was racing through his head now would be quite different! It would be win-win both for him *and* Stavros's downtrodden English daughter!

He set it out rapidly and concisely—frankly—in a cool, clear, businesslike manner.

'We marry—without delay—so your father will finally give the go-ahead I'm seeking and commit to the merger. Thereafter it will take about half a year for the merger to be completed. There are legal aspects, financial checks, due diligence, staffing issues, regulatory conditions that must be met.' He reeled off the list. 'As well as organisational conditions that I want to put in place. These things are seldom simple and never speedy. So we stay married for the duration and then—and *only* then—when the merger is irreversible, and I have what I want…'

His expression changed.

'Then we simply divorce and go our separate ways. The payoff for me is that I get the merger I want—it's ideal for my business—and you…' He drew a breath. 'You get a handsome divorce settlement from me by way of a thank-you for enabling me to get my business merger. You can pick up your life again—go back to England, do whatever you want.'

He took another breath, levelling his eyes intently on her, making her understand what he was promising her.

'You will never know poverty again.'

His eyes didn't let hers go. He was willing her to see what he was seeing. Willing her to agree. To say yes.

And even as he waited for her reaction he knew, with a searing awareness that he had been trying to silence ever since his car had glided to a halt beside her bowed figure, storming away from the Coustakis mansion with her hopeless dreams in tatters, that there was a whole other reason why he had proposed what he had.

His eyes rested on her…on the beauty that had been revealed to him…the beauty he could not now forget. Could not pass by…

There was a truth about her he could not deny—a truth that had been blazing in him like a fire that could not be quenched. It was flaring again now, as she sat opposite him, gazing at him incredulously with those luminous wide-set grey-green eyes, so incredibly beautiful…

I want her—I desire her. Since the moment she revealed her amazing beauty to me in all its radiance I have known that. I thought I had to ignore it, suppress it, because I refused to play Stavros's infernal games! But if she can be persuaded to what I am urging her now... I can indulge in my desire for her! She can be mine!

Six months, he'd said. Well, that was all his amours ever lasted anyway. After that they always burned out, became stale and tedious. No woman he'd desired had ever lasted longer and he preferred it that way—he freely admitted that.

Six months would get him everything he wanted! It would guarantee a business merger that would double the Lakaris fortune, just as his father had intended, and, as a sweetener like no other, this stunningly beautiful woman he could not take his eyes from would be his for the duration.

What more could he possibly want?

The question was rhetorical—the answer was blazing in his head.

All he needed was her agreement, and his eyes willed her to give him the answer he sought…

Rosalie heard what he was saying—heard his words, though she could scarcely credit them—but it was the last of them that was echoing in her head as he fell silent.

'You will never know poverty again.'

She swallowed. Looked about her. The swish restaurant they were lunching at was filled now with diners, all well heeled. Waiters hovered discreetly, taking orders for the delicious gourmet food that was the everyday fare of those who frequented places like this.

She shifted position in her chair, feeling the soft fabric of the outfit she was wearing—remembered the price tag that had been on it. It would have been as impossible for her to buy on her cleaning wages as buying a villa in the Caribbean…

Memory plunged through her of the last two days… the night she'd spent at that five-star London hotel, the luxury and the lavishness of it all. The fortune it had cost.

Her eyes went back to the man sitting opposite her with his unreadable expression, waiting for her response.

She looked at the superb cut of his business suit easing across his broad shoulders, the silk tie, the gold tie-pin, the svelte look of sleek, expensive grooming about him…thought back to the low, lean car he'd driven her here in, with its famous logo on the bonnet and the deep soft leather bucket seats she'd sunk into. Thought back to the flight in first class she'd taken to Athens, the non-stop champagne, the hovering flight attendants, the very lap of luxury…

She'd tasted that world—that luxury—glimpsed like a tantalising marsh-light what might have been hers had her father been the kind of father she'd woven such futile hopes and longings around…

But because those hopes and longings had crashed and burned, all she could do now was go back to London—back to the life she had there…all she'd ever have.

A sick feeling of dread and deep reluctance filled her.

Can I face it? Can I truly face it? Once my anger and my hurt and my outrage have worn off? Once I'm back in that dump of a bedsit, listening to the addicts and the drunks in the other bedsits? Hearing the endless traffic in the street, smelling the damp in the walls...spending my days slogging to clean up other people's filth and my nights trying to stay awake to study, because study is the only hope I have of escaping from the life my father's callousness has condemned me to...

The grim, bleak life she would be condemned to again.

Unless...

CHAPTER SIX

SHE FELT HER hands clench in her lap. Made herself look at the man who had just said what he had said. His eyes were resting on her, his expression veiled. He was waiting for her to answer him.

'So,' Alexandros Lakaris said, his voice level, eyes resting on her still, 'what do you say?'

She couldn't answer him. Not yet. Too much was in her head. He seemed to realise that, because his expression changed, became less intent. He was backing off. Giving her space.

She saw him sit back, pour himself more coffee.

'It's a lot to take in—for both of us.'

There was a smoothness in his voice now, and the slightest masking of the expression in his amazingly dark deep eyes. Eyes which she was all too aware she just wanted to go on gazing into, despite all the tumult in her beleaguered mind.

How easy it would be, she found herself thinking, just to go on looking into them…letting all the stormy emotions twisting inside her subside, letting herself just fall into that dark, gold-flecked gaze…

How tempting…

But he was continuing, easing his shoulders, reaching for his refilled coffee cup. 'So what I suggest is this. Don't rush back to London just yet. Stay tonight, at the very least, in Athens. I'll book you into a hotel at *my* expense,' he emphasised, 'because it's only fair that you have enough time to think about your answer.'

He drained his coffee and got to his feet, holding out his hand to her. 'Come—let's get some fresh air. A stroll by the sea will do us both good.' His mouth twisted wryly. 'It's been a strenuous two days—and an emotional roller coaster for you.'

She let him draw her up, because it seemed easier to do so, let him fold her hand into the crook of his arm and pat it with brief reassurance. He led her out of the restaurant, pausing only to settle the bill with a flick of a gold-trimmed credit card. Then they were out on the pavement, and he was guiding her across the road to the seafront.

The warm sun was like a blessing on her, and she felt its benediction on her confused, exhausted emotions as they strolled along.

Alexandros Lakaris was pointing out a couple of islands visible out to sea, mentioning how the bay had once, in Athens's Classical Golden Age, been the scene of the famous battle of Salamis against Persian invaders, telling her about Greece's struggles so long ago.

Rosalie listened, glad of the diversion from her turbid thoughts and emotions, finding herself interested in what he was saying. She knew so little about Greece, ancient or modern…

But it's my heritage—just as much as my English heritage! A heritage I've been denied. And even if my father is a man to deplore and be ashamed of, that doesn't mean I have to reject everything about this side of me!

She felt her gaze flick from the seascape to the man at her side, as they strolled along the promenade in the afternoon warmth. Strolling along as if they were already a couple…

But it's absurd what he's suggested, isn't it? Surely it is?

Her thoughts swirled within her, impossible to make sense of. All she knew right now was that somehow, and she did not know how, it seemed to be so very easy, so very relaxed, to be walking along like this, in a leisurely fashion, with his tall figure beside her matching his steps to hers.

He took them to the start of the marina.

'Do you have a yacht?' Rosalie heard herself asking, looking at all the boats bobbing on the water.

He shook his head. 'A dinghy,' he said. 'I keep it moored at Kallistris.'

'Kallistris?'

'My island.'

Rosalie's eyes widened. 'Your *island*? You have an *island*? A whole island to yourself?'

He looked amused. 'It's a very small island,' he said. 'But it is my favourite place on earth.'

His expression changed and she lifted her eyes to his. There had been emotion in his voice—deep emotion.

'Tell me about it,' she heard herself say.

They resumed their stroll, walking along the edge of the quay on old cobbles, near the water lapping and slapping against the hulls of the moored yachts.

'It's reachable by helicopter and I go there whenever I can,' Alexandros Lakaris was saying.

His voice warmed with fond affection—she could hear it. 'There's very little on it. Goats, mostly! And an old fisherman's cottage by the beach, done up as a villa now. There's a smallholding inland, where Panos and Maria live—they look after the place for me. It's very peaceful.'

'It sounds lovely,' Rosalie said wistfully.

A whole island all to yourself, set in this azure sea, beneath this golden sun... A world, a universe away from the squalid back streets of the East End.

'So, what would you like to do now?' Alexandros Lakaris was asking her as they reached the far side of the quay. 'Shall we go for a drive? And then back into Athens?'

She gave a nod. It was easier to let him make the decisions, easier to go with the flow.

Maybe it would be sensible to spend one more night here. To at least think over what he's thrown at me.

Was it really as absurd as it sounded? When the alternative was so grim… When she'd had a brief, tantalising taste of the kind of luxurious life she could enjoy for months and months if she went with what he'd so extraordinarily suggested.

And at the end of those months she could go back to England with the divorce settlement he was promising her after he'd got the merger he wanted.

Into her head sprang visions of the kind of life she could lead if she did not have to go back to the bleak, exhausting slog she'd come from.

I could get out of London! Move to the country or a beautiful cathedral town! Or even the seaside. Make a completely new life for myself! A life of my own choosing.

The vision hovered in her head. So incredibly tempting…

They reached the car and he opened the passenger door for her. As he did so, he paused, frowning, as if something had just struck him.

'Where is your luggage? All the clothes you bought?'

Rosalie's face hardened as she got into her seat and he did likewise, gunning the powerful engine.

'I left them,' she said. 'And I wish to God I didn't have to wear this outfit either! I'll be sending it back to him from London.'

She heard Alexandros Lakaris say something in Greek. She thought he must be swearing, so perhaps that was just as well.

'I'll have them fetched for you,' he said, his face grim with displeasure as he moved off into the roadway. He turned to her. 'Would it persuade you to keep them if you knew that in fact it was me who paid for them? I was going to charge them to your father, but in the circumstances…'

'I can't accept them from you either!' Rosalie exclaimed hotly. 'How could you think I would?'

'If you accept my proposal, then of course you can,' he replied. 'In fact,' he went on, 'you'll need many more.' He glanced across at her and there was that glint in his eye again. It did things to her that it shouldn't. 'As my wife,' he said, 'you would be superbly dressed…'

She made a face, trying not to see herself let loose in yet more gorgeous designer departments. 'Is that supposed to persuade me?' she posed.

'Will it?' he countered.

She shook her head. 'I mustn't let it,' she answered in a low voice, looking down at her lap. She gave a sigh, then looked at him straight, took a breath. 'Mr Lakaris, if—'

He cut her off with a frown. 'I think we have gone long beyond the stage of formal address,' he said wryly. 'My friends,' he went on, 'call me Xandros.'

'Well, whatever I call you,' she persisted, 'I have to be absolutely sure that I'm not…not…letting you buy me things. Expensive clothes. Expensive hotel rooms. Expensive meals, come to that…'

He frowned. 'You were happy enough to buy clothes when you thought your father was paying.'

'That's different—he's my father. But you'd be—'

'Your husband,' he supplied. 'And you, as I set out at lunchtime, would be my wife,' he went on, and there was a crispness in his voice that she could hear clearly. 'A wife who is enabling me to make a *lot* of money, thanks to this merger!' He glanced at her briefly. 'Does that reassure you at all?'

'I suppose so,' she said uneasily.

'Good,' he replied decisively. 'And now…' he changed gear and the powerful car shot forward, before settling into a fast cruising speed along the highway '…let's put all that aside for the time being. Tell me—how do you fancy driving out to Sounion? There's an ancient temple there, and a dramatic headland. Let me show you something of Greece. If a couture wardrobe can't tempt you to marry me, maybe Greece will!'

She heard humour in his voice, and he threw her a slanting smile.

His eyes went back to the road ahead, but Rosalie's did not do likewise. That brief smile, crinkling his eyes and curving his sculpted mouth, had made her stomach flip.

Her gaze focussed on his strong, perfectly carved profile, the fine blade of his nose, the chiselled jaw, the faint furrow of concentration on his broad brow as he overtook a lorry and then eased his square long-fingered hands on the steering wheel again. She took in the breadth of his shoulders, the long, lean length of him—the whole incredible package of honed masculinity that was Alexandros Lakaris—and she was unable to tear her gaze away.

She was helpless to stop her father's jibing words echoing in her head.

'You'd be the envy of every woman in Athens!'

Galling though it was, how could she deny the truth of that jibing taunt her father had lanced at her? For she knew, with a burning consciousness, that when it came to temptation Alexandros Lakaris, all six feet of drop-dead gorgeousness, was in a league of his own…

She dragged her thoughts away, her eyes away.

If they married on the terms he'd set out—*if!*—then that factor, above all, was not a good reason.

In her head his words hovered again—his promise to her.

'You will never know poverty again...'

Temptation like an overpowering wave swept over her. She could marry this incredible-looking man, enjoy his wealth, revel in the lifestyle that would have been hers had her father not been as callous, as heartless, as despicable as he was. And she could walk away at the end of it all with a passport to a better life for herself.

I could do it! I really could do it!

But would she? That was the question she must answer.

And it hung in her head like a burning brand.

* * *

Xandros glanced expectantly towards the entrance to the hotel's rooftop restaurant. He'd phoned through to Rosalie's room and she was on her way. He was glad she had accepted his suggestion that they have dinner together tonight, glad she'd let him book her into this hotel in central Athens, and glad that she hadn't insisted, after all, on him driving her to the airport so she could fly back to London.

And he was glad, above all, that at least she hadn't blown his proposal out of the water.

Because the more he considered it, the more ideal it became. In his head he ran through all the reasons why one more time as he took a sip from the gin-based cocktail he'd been served as he waited for Rosalie.

Just as he'd told her that afternoon, all the financial reasons stacked up irrefutably. And so did his own personal reasons. Reasons that, as he caught sight of her hovering a little hesitantly at the restaurant entrance, seared across his retinas.

His gaze was riveted on her as she walked towards him, guided by the maître d'.

A swift phone call to the Coustakis mansion as they'd headed back from Sounion at the end of the afternoon had resulted in her two new suitcases full of designer clothes being delivered to the hotel by the time they reached it. And clearly, in the hours since she'd checked in, she'd taken her pick of the contents.

To very good effect.

His eyes swept over her, warming with rich appreciation. An LBD—classic style—skimmed her tall, slender body flawlessly. She wore it with an evening jacket lightly embroidered in silver thread, adorned with a long silver necklace and matching bracelets. Her hair was upswept, which lengthened her graceful neck, enhancing an elegance that was rounded off by high heels that gave her an amazing sashaying walk as she approached.

Thee mou, but she was beautiful! To think she had clutched that damnable bucket and mop and scrubbed filthy floors!

Even as he thought about it, another thought gelled in his mind.

She never will again—never!

Whatever it took to convince her to accept his proposal, he would do it. She deserved no less.

And nor do I.

He felt that low-frequency purring start inside him as she came up to him. This beautiful woman, whose existence he had known of for only four days, had blown him away.

He got to his feet, greeting her warmly, letting the glow in his eyes show his appreciation of her.

It was having an effect, he could see—the very effect he wanted.

She wasn't impervious to him—he knew that with absolute certainty. He'd seen that revealing flare in her eyes, try to conceal it as she might. And when they'd been in London he had sensed, with his very well-honed male instinct and his considerable experience of her sex, that she was as appreciative of him as he was of her, however offhand her manner had been.

But that initial deliberate indifference to him—caused, he thought ruefully, by his own guarded behaviour towards her, because he'd been unwilling to disabuse her about her father and unwilling to admit to himself how drawn he was to her—was all gone now. There was no longer any need for it.

He felt the purring inside him heighten. Now they could give their sensual awareness of each other full rein.

It was there right now—he could tell—in that flaring of her pupils as he smiled in welcome. In the flaring that was echoed in his own eyes. In the quickening of his pulse…

Impulse took over. An unstoppable urge. Without full consciousness of what he was doing, only male instinct possessing him, he caught her hand, rested his other hand lightly on her slender waist.

'You look fantastic!' he breathed. His voice was husky, again unconsciously—he couldn't help it. His eyes moved over her face, taking in just how exquisitely lovely she looked, gazing at him now, wide-eyed, unconsciously inviting…

That low-frequency purr intensified. Became irresistible…

His mouth dipped to hers…

It was the lightest of kisses—the softest brushing of his mouth on hers, lasting only seconds. The merest fleeting sensation…the merest sip of the honey of her silken lips… The kind of kiss any man could greet any woman with in public.

And yet he had to use every ounce of his self-control to draw back from her, to smile down at her and release her hand, her waist, help her to take a seat. He could see that her face had flushed, her colour heightened and the low purring inside him was glad of this visible evidence of her response to him.

Of his to her he needed no second proof. Desire

rushed through him. And an absolute certainty that the half-crazy idea he had blurted out to her that afternoon to stop her fleeing back to London, to the grim, bleak life she lived there—the impulsive offer that, despite his original determination to have nothing to do whatsoever with Stavros's English daughter, had seemed the most obvious thing to make—was, in fact, the one idea he longed to make happen… He wanted to make her his.

He resumed his own seat, his eyes never leaving her. Her gaze had dipped and she was busying herself smoothing a napkin over her lap, the colour gradually subsiding from her flushed cheeks. Xandros knew he needed to put her at ease with him. There would be time enough to make clear to her just how he felt…

'I thought it best to dine here at the hotel,' he opened. 'The food is excellent and I thought you might like the view.'

He gestured to the picture windows, which opened on to a terrace beyond. He heard her breath catch with delight as she looked past him to see what he was indicating: the ultimate symbol of Athens, spotlit as it always was by night.

'The Acropolis!' she breathed, with wonder in her voice, leaning forward to maximise her view.

'And the Parthenon on top of it,' he supplied.

Her face had lit up, enhancing her beauty, and as she gazed at the vista Xandros gazed at her face. One thought only blazed in him: whatever it took to convince her to accept his proposal, he must do it.

He could tell that her presence here with him was drawing eyes. Not because he was dining with a beautiful woman—Athens society was well used to that—but because up until recently the woman he'd been dining with had been Ariadne Coustakis.

And that, he realised, thinking it through rapidly, was yet another bonus to be gained from going through with the plan that he'd put to Stavros's English daughter that afternoon.

It will give me a highly acceptable explanation for why my relationship with Ariadne is no more. A totally unexpected coup de foudre when I met her half-sister led her to release me from our engagement.

The tale would play well, and it would silence any speculation arising from his precipitate marriage to another woman. He did not want Rosalie to be the butt of gossip.

He realised she was talking.

'It looks so close…the Acropolis!'

'It's quite some distance away, really—it looks close because there are no high-rise buildings between here and it,' he replied. 'Many buildings have a view over it— my apartment does,' he said.

He started to tell her about the extensive ruins of classical times, both on the Acropolis and at its base, and then went on to describe some of the geography of the city itself—the different areas from Plaka to Syntagma Square.

She listened with interest, asking questions, increasingly relaxed as their dinner arrived, sipping at her wine.

'I must buy myself a guide book,' she said. A shadow crossed her face. 'It seems sad that I know absolutely nothing about a city that I should have known all my life—'

She broke off, took another mouthful of her wine.

'It isn't too late to learn to love your Greek heritage,' Xandros said quietly.

He left it at that—let the thought gel, take root. He left unspoken, for now, the corollary... *If you marry me...*

Throughout dinner he kept the conversation and the mood casual, easily friendly, and it served his purpose well. For all the privations of her deprived upbringing she was obviously not unintelligent—just ignorant of a great deal of what he took for granted. But she held her own, asked good questions, showed a sensitivity that he appreciated.

'I know there's a fuss about the Elgin Marbles being in the British Museum,' she ventured, 'but I don't really understand why.'

'Because,' Xandros informed her sternly, 'they are not the "Elgin" Marbles at all—they are the *Parthenon* Marbles! The problem is,' he went on, 'that Lord Elgin acquired them in good faith—but from an authority that did not own them in the first place. From the Ottoman government of Greece at the time.'

She wrinkled her brow. 'Ottoman...?'

'The foreign empire from Asia Minor that conquered the Middle East and the ancient Byzantine Empire in the fifteenth century—and ruled Greece for four hundred years until we finally shook them off! It was a dark time for Greece. A dark time,' he added, 'for my family.'

She looked at him questioningly.

'My family goes back a long way,' he supplied. 'Back to the Byzantine Empire itself—the empire that succeeded the Roman Empire at the start of the Dark Ages for Western Europe. Here in the east the light of civilisation continued to burn, and the Byzantine capital,

Constantinople—modern-day Istanbul—was one of the greatest cities on earth!'

She frowned, and he realised he needed to explain something more to her.

'It's because my family can trace its roots so far back,' he said, choosing his words carefully, 'that your father—who, by his own admission, is a completely self-made man—is so keen on marrying *his* family into it.'

He saw Rosalie's expression change.

'He threw it at me,' she said. 'The fact that I would be marrying "a lordly Lakaris".'

Xandros's mouth twisted. 'Was that before or after he threatened to throw you out, still as penniless as he'd deliberately kept you all your life, if you didn't do what he wanted?'

He shook his head, dismissing his own question. If Stavros's daughter married him it would not be at her father's bidding—let alone because of his financial blackmail.

'But we don't need to consider your father at all,' he said with a dismissive shrug. 'After the despicable way he's treated you he deserves no consideration! What we do is our business—not his.'

He saw Rosalie's expression flicker momentarily, and then a questioning look in her eye.

'Are you really "lordly"?' she asked.

Did her question indicate reservations? Xandros shook his head again. 'Not for centuries!' he said lightly. 'The Byzantine Empire ceased to exist over five hundred years ago!'

She frowned again. 'I thought there was a king of Greece at some time. Isn't there a royal family somewhere?'

'In exile,' Xandros explained. 'But it was never actually Greek. The family is an offshoot of the Danish royal family, installed when Greece got its freedom from the Ottomans in the nineteenth century. There are links to the last of the Byzantine imperial dynasties, but very distant. Not involving my family at all.'

It seemed irrelevant to add that during the era of the Greek monarchy his forebears had been courtiers—those times were long gone now. His thoughts darkened. Besides, it had been during the final post-war phase of the monarchy that his grandfather, with close personal links to the royals, had lived so extravagantly and recklessly, creating a financial precipice that had nearly bankrupted the family.

As his grandson, he was still intent on ensuring such danger would never again threaten the Lakaris fortunes. And it was that intention that was the driver for this Coustakis merger that his father had recommended as the best way forward. The lucrative merger to which the exquisitely beautiful woman opposite him was now key.

It will work—the plan that I have come up with! It will placate Stavros, convince him to agree to the merger. It won't tie me permanently in marriage, and yet it will give me all the time I want with this most desirable of women...

Now all he had to do was convince her to accept him and claim her for his own…

CHAPTER SEVEN

ROSALIE STIRRED, STRETCHING her limbs in the wide bed, waking slowly. She had slept so much better than on that night of nerve-racked tossing and turning she had spent in that over-gilded bed in her father's over-gilded mansion. Then, her dreams had been fitful, filled with seesawing hopes and apprehension. But last night they had been very different.

They had been filled not with anxious imaginings of her forthcoming encounter with her long-lost father, which bitter reality had sent crashing and burning into oblivion, but with memories of the afternoon she had spent with Alexandros Lakaris.

And their evening together.

And his kiss on greeting her…

She felt a melting within her as memory replayed that moment—how his mouth had dipped to hers, brushing with exquisite lightness the tender swell of her lips.

So brief…so magical…

And so entirely unexpected.

Because nothing in his behaviour towards her till that moment had given her cause to think that he was thinking of her in those terms.

Oh, she'd seen the stunned expression on his face when she'd sailed out of that hotel restaurant in London, glitzed to the hilt after her shopping spree. And it had been gratifying not to be Little Miss Invisible to him any more, after his obvious disdain for the way she'd looked when he'd found her.

But after complimenting her on her improved appearance—it would have been difficult for him to have ignored the difference all those beauty treatments and a designer outfit had made to her!—he'd reverted to his earlier attitude: impersonal to the point of indifferent. And he'd clearly been glad to be shot of her when he'd dropped her off at her father's house and driven off immediately.

But she'd been wrong about him. Quite wrong.

More memory pushed into her head. How she'd sobbed all over him in her rage and misery when he'd found her fleeing her father's house the next day...how comforting he'd been. How kind and sympathetic. She heard his words again, as he explained to her just why he'd brought her to Athens, how shocked he'd been to find her living the way she'd had to in London.

'How could I leave you there like that?' he'd said.

She felt her throat tighten.

I thought him brusque and uncaring—but he isn't! He isn't at all.

There was a warmth in him she had never suspected. Just as she had never expected that kiss last evening.

Memory came full circle and it played again in her head, tantalising and beguiling...

But had it meant anything?

It was just a kiss in public. He probably kisses every

woman he dines with. Especially a woman he wants to persuade to marry him.

And there it was—centre-stage in her head—the one thing she had to think about. Marrying Alexandros Lakaris for six months to their mutual financial benefit.

Emotions, thoughts, churned inside her. Could she really do it? Do what Xandros was urging her to do?

She lay there, staring up at the ceiling, thinking through the implications. For six months she would be Alexandros Lakaris's wife—dressed up to the nines, enjoying the kind of luxury she had never dreamt would come her way in all her life! She would be living here in Greece, exploring the heritage she had never known.

Suddenly there was a bleakness in her eyes. She would not have a chance to get to know that heritage if she went back to her poverty-stricken life in London. How long would it take her to earn enough money to come back to Athens? Even when she eventually got a half-decent job once she had some qualifications?

Her expression shadowed. This time yesterday she had thought it would be through her father that she would experience her Greek heritage. Now it might be through Xandros.

And would that be unwelcome?

The answer was there as soon as she asked the question. Of course not! How could it be?

She knew now that he was far kinder than she'd originally thought him, and angered on her behalf by her father's callousness. That must surely warm her towards him. Plus, she knew simply from the time she'd spent with him so far that he was easy to be with, interesting to talk to, good-humoured and well-informed—without being in the least patronising about her lack of knowledge in things he took for granted thanks to his privileged background.

And then, of course, there was the most obvious, inescapable fact of all about how it would be if she accepted the extraordinary proposal he'd made to her.

The fact that a single glance from those incredible, dark, gold-flecked, long-lashed eyes of his could make her pulse race in ways she had never known… The fact that she just wanted to gaze and gaze at his absolute male perfection…drink in everything about him…

And how could she not be smitten with her limited experience? It had always been difficult, even impossible, looking after her poor, frail mother as she had, to have any kind of social life…any kind of romance… How could anyone compare with Xandros?

From the very first she had acknowledged his searing impact on her. How could it be otherwise? He was the stuff of dreams, of fantasies… But could she—would she—make them real?

And would *he*?

If she were really to go ahead and marry him, then what would he expect? Or want…? What would *she* want?

Even as she formed the questions the answers were there, in the quickening of her blood as she replayed, yet again, the soft, sensuous touch of his mouth on hers. It had engendered within her an ache, a yearning for something more… Oh, so much more!

The phone beside her bed started to ring, interrupting her hectic thoughts. She picked it up. It was Xandros.

'Hi,' he said.

His voice was warm and friendly. And good to hear.

'Have you had breakfast yet? If not, how about brunch by the hotel pool? In half an hour?'

'So...' Xandros eyed her carefully as they sat at a table in the poolside bistro. 'Do you think you've reached a decision yet?'

He didn't want to pressurise her, but...

I want her to say yes.

Watching her, he was glad he was wearing sunglasses, for it gave him the opportunity to study her without her being aware of it. He was even more sure of what he wanted. He hadn't seen her yet in leisurewear, and now that he was it was every bit as rewarding as seeing her in more formal daywear and evening wear.

The short, above-the-knee sundress in a swirling pattern of yellow and blue, its halter neck exposing her graceful shoulders, looked good on her. More than good. Her hair was not upswept this morning, but pulled back into a simple ponytail, and the long, lush sweep of it curved over her bare shoulder. She was wearing make-up, but minimal—just mascara, a trace of eyeliner and lip gloss. She looked fresh, natural...and breathtakingly lovely.

His mind went back to the way she'd looked that first day—with dirt smeared on her face and hollows under her eyes, fatigue in every line of her body.

Never again—never!

She hadn't answered him and he stilled, watching her. He could see the expressions moving in her eyes, her lips pressing together as if she were nerving herself to speak. He saw her swallow.

'Do *you* still want to go ahead?' she asked. Her voice was low—diffident, even.

'If you're asking if I've changed my mind, the answer is no,' Xandros said firmly. He paused, then said what he thought she needed to hear right now, softening his voice, seeking to reassure her. 'It will work out. I promise you. You won't regret it. I'll make sure of that.'

He gave a wry, quirking smile, wondering off-hand how many other women of his acquaintance would have been so hesitant about accepting an invitation to marry him…

Then he sobered. Yes, well…Rosalie's half-sister hadn't been that keen, had she?

Even thinking about Ariadne made him feel all over again that underlying sense of relief he'd experienced when he'd read her text. His eyes rested now on her half-sister. He wondered how he could ever have truly imagined himself capable of marrying Ariadne…

She was beautiful, yes, but never—not once—had he felt that low purring desire go through him the way it was doing now, yet again, as he sat eating brunch with Rosalie.

She was who he desired… And if she said yes now—as he hoped beyond hope she was about to do—then his desire would be richly fulfilled…

He let his gaze continue to rest on her, waiting to see what she would say. 'Do you need more time?' he asked, searching her face.

She gave a quick shake of her head. 'No—no, that wouldn't help. I…I've thought it all through. I can't really think more than I've thought already.'

Was there a slight flush to her cheeks as she spoke? A momentary dip in her gaze? His eyes stayed on her. He was waiting for her next words. Urging her to say them, and for them to be the ones he wanted to hear.

'So?' he prompted.

He felt the world was holding its breath. *He* was holding his breath. He saw her swallow again, inhale. Lift her chin. Look right at him. Give him a quick, decisive nod.

'Let's do it!' she said.

The words rushed from her, as if she might suddenly change her mind. But he would give her no chance to do so—*none.*

He reached for her hand, took it in his. Held it fast. 'Good call,' he said.

Satisfaction rushed through him, his mood soaring. And why should it not? He was getting what he wanted—*everything* he wanted! She was his. Life had never seemed better, nor the bright sun brighter.

He couldn't wait to make her his wife...

'Do you like it?' Xandros's voice was enquiring.

Rosalie stared at the ring on her finger, glittering with diamonds.

Was this real? Had she really said yes to the idea Alexandros Lakaris had put to her less than twenty-four hours ago?

Should I have taken more time to give him my answer?

But she'd thought it through, and through, and through. Either she said yes or she went back to her grim, bleak, poverty-stricken life in the East End of London. And she couldn't face that—not now! Not when she'd had a glimpse of escape from it, a taste of what luxury felt like. It might be venal to look at it like that, but that was easy to say if you were rich...

The diamonds scintillated in the lights of the very

exclusive jewellers she and Xandros were in. Emotion caught at her.

Mum would have loved to see this day! See this ring on my finger! She would be glad for me—thrilled for me!

That was what she must think. No one—not even her monstrous father!—would be harmed by what she was going to do. Both he and Xandros would be richer and so, in six months' time, would she. Oh, not rich like them, but rich enough to escape for ever from the bleakness of her London life.

Mum would want that for me—I know she would!

'If you don't like this ring there are plenty more to choose from,' Xandros was saying now.

She looked up at him. 'It's fabulous!' she said. 'If you think it's necessary?' she added doubtfully, knowing how horrendously expensive a ring like this must be.

'Yes, it is,' Xandros replied firmly. 'People will expect it.' He gave her a pointed look. 'Rosalie, this marriage has to look genuine. I mean, it *will* be genuine, but there can't be any questions about it, okay? So, like it or not, you'll have to endure wearing it!'

His tone was light, good humoured, but she got the message. Kyria Lakaris-to-be had to look the part—right down to the priceless engagement ring now weighing upon her finger.

She felt its weight as they made their next stop—the register office—to set in motion the process of enabling them to marry. She would need her birth certificate, she discovered, and Xandros undertook to have it couriered out to Athens. The wedding would take place as soon as possible and Xandros—thankfully—had allayed the chief of her alarms.

'We'll keep it completely private—no guests. Not even family, okay?'

She was relieved. Having her father present would have been unendurable. Xandros had already told her that *he* would deal with him—she would not have to see him or have anything to do with him.

'I'll let him think that after throwing your tantrum yesterday—because that's the way he'll see it!—I've prevailed upon you to see the sense of what he said.' Xandros had told her over brunch, his expression taut. 'The rest is true enough—that I've whisked you away, put you up in a hotel and am now planning our wedding with all speed. As for my own interests in this…' His tone had taken on an edge that had been audible. 'I'll be making it crystal clear to him that the wedding *only* goes ahead once I have his commitment—in writing—to the merger, and a promise that active negotiations to that end will start immediately. He will give me leave to proceed with due diligence and all the other matters the merger will require, and he will co-operate fully with all the legal processes.'

There were 'legal processes' between her and Xandros, too, that had to be addressed. Their next port of call was his private lawyer's office, where Rosalie's only protest was at how much money Xandros had stipulated in the pre-nup was to be paid in the event of their divorce—a divorce that was not going to be an 'if' but a 'when'.

'It's far too much!' she protested as they left.

He looked across at her. 'Rosalie, don't argue. If you want me to show you just how much my annual profits are projected to increase once the merger with your father goes ahead, then I shall. I am going to be a much richer man than I am now! Your payoff is worth every penny, I promise you!'

She subsided, but with an uneasy sigh. So much money… When she had been so poor…

She felt his hand take hers, as if he sensed her unease.

'It will be okay,' he said.

The warmth in his voice was reassuring, and reassurance, Rosalie discovered, was what she needed over the coming days.

She was to go on staying at the hotel until they married, when she would move in with Xandros. He took her to see his apartment, so she could get used to it, and she gazed about her at the spacious expanse and clean lines.

'Not too minimalist?' he asked.

She shook her head. It seemed very…*intimate*…to be here with him, alone in his apartment. Yet his manner towards her was exactly as it was in public—friendly and easy-going. Just that. She was glad, because it made her comfortable to be with him, but at the same time…

She watched him pick up a pile of personal post and leaf through it, busying himself opening an array of envelopes. She wandered off, not wanting to distract him, glancing into the formidably equipped kitchen before discovering the bedrooms. There were three—two guests and a clear master. She stood in the doorway for a moment, her expression uncertain.

Would it be her bedroom as well as his?

A quiver of uncertainty went through her. Since that first evening when they'd dined together he had not kissed her again—not even a peck on the cheek to say hello or farewell. She felt a strange little tug around her heart. Part of her wanted to ask him just what kind of marriage theirs was going to be, however brief—but part of her could not bring herself to do so.

Because in the end did it matter? Did it matter that he was the most fantastic-looking man she'd ever set eyes on? That since that kiss at the restaurant she had felt an ache, a yearning, that he had awoken in her with that brief touch of his lips on hers?

That wasn't the reason they were marrying! That was what she had to remember. The reasons they were going to marry were financial—nothing more than that. And if that was all Xandros wanted of their brief marriage then she must accept it.

Except that strange little tug around her heart came again… No man, she knew, would ever set her pulse racing, bring the colour to her cheeks, make her so blazingly aware of her own body…of his…

Her eyes went to the huge double bed in the master bedroom. Wide enough for two…wide and inviting… But would she ever be invited into it…? Uncertainty mixed within her with yearning…longing…

'Here you are!'

Xandros's voice was warm as it sounded behind her. Rosalie turned.

'Seen everything?' he asked.

For a second his eyes rested on her with an expression she could not quite make out. Then it was gone. He was speaking again.

'I've been going through the post—mostly invitations! But we'll ignore them all until we're safely married. Then,' he said, and his eyes washed over her, 'I'll start showing you off. I'm looking forward to it!'

Rosalie felt herself colouring, confusion filling her

again. Was it just that he wanted her to look her best for his friends and acquaintances? To show the world—and convince her father—how real their marriage was? He could afford no hint that it would be over and done with before the year was out, leaving Xandros with what he wanted—the merger with her father—and herself with a hefty divorce payout?

Is that all our marriage is going to be about?

She turned away, feeling that strange tug of emotion coming again, and stepped back into the wide corridor, then into the triple-aspect reception room, her feet taking her towards the view of the Parthenon on the Acropolis. She paused to gaze out over it, still feeling that strange tug of emotion.

Hands closed lightly over her shoulders and she felt Xandros behind her, his breath warm on her neck. Her own breath caught, feeling him so close, catching the spiced scent of his aftershave… She wanted to lean back into him, feel his arms go around her waist to embrace her, but she was too unsure to move.

'It's a good sight, isn't it?' he murmured softly.

She gave a slow nod, conscious not of the ancient monument but only of his hands upon her. For a moment—just a moment—she felt his touch tighten, as if he would turn her to him. As if he would take her into his arms…

Then, instead, he merely grazed the top of her head with the lightest and most fraternal of kisses, his hands dropping away.

'I'll run you back to your hotel,' he said.

There was nothing in his voice but his usual easygoing manner.

With a flickering smile of acquiescence Rosalie let him usher her out of his apartment, outwardly serene.

But inside, she knew, she was conscious of a sense of disappointment. Of a creeping melancholy.

She had no business feeling that way. No right at all.

But she did, all the same.

Xandros was visiting his mother. He didn't want to, but he owed her that at least. He'd had to make a difficult phone call to her before he'd flown to London, telling her as carefully as he could that Ariadne had pulled out of their engagement.

'But *why*?' his mother had cried, dismayed. 'I thought it was all agreed!'

'So did I,' he'd said. 'But there it is. I have to respect her decision.'

He knew his mother was upset. She had wanted him to marry Ariadne, the daughter of her childhood friend—to marry her and achieve the merger her husband had urged his son to make as a sure way to increase the Lakaris fortunes he had worked so hard to rescue. She had wanted him to marry and give her grandchildren, to cheer her widowhood and to continue the ancient line to which he had been born, of which he was now the sole representative since the untimely death of his father three years ago.

And if Ariadne had been the perfect bride for him in his mother's eyes, Xandros knew with foreboding that she would deplore his sudden decision to marry Ariadne's illegitimate English half-sister instead.

Which was why he had to visit her in person—to explain the precise reasons for his precipitate action.

As he had expected, she did deplore it—and vocally.

'Xandros, who *is* this girl? Nobody! You can't possibly be thinking that she can be a substitute for Ariadne!'

'That is precisely what I *don't* think!' he answered. He took a breath and looked into his mother's eyes, which held a troubled expression. 'She understands my reasons and agrees it will only be a temporary arrangement. And…' he took another breath '…this won't just be for my benefit. I want to do this for *her*,' he said feelingly. 'She's had a wretched life. Coustakis never acknowledged her existence. He condemned both her and her mother to lifelong poverty. She deserves better!'

His mother looked at him, her expression still troubled. 'Are you sure?' she asked slowly. 'Are you sure that you know what you're doing, Xandros?'

He looked at her straight. 'Yes,' he said. 'And it is very, very simple, I promise you.'

She looked as if she was going to say something more, but he forestalled her. He did not want their conversation moving on to any other aspect of just why he was going through with this marriage—that it was precisely *because* it was going to be temporary that it appealed to him, and that as soon as he was free of it, his desire for Rosalie slaked, he would resume the carefree, unattached bachelor lifestyle his mother considered a waste of his time.

He changed the subject away from marrying Rosalie and the reasons he was doing so.

'Tell me, have you heard anything from Ariadne? Her mobile phone isn't working. Coustakis must have cancelled it—he's vindictive enough to do that, after disowning her as he has! My guess is she's gone to stay with her maternal grandmother's relatives in Scotland. But I don't know their whereabouts, or even their name.'

His mother shook her head. 'I have heard nothing from Ariadne either. I try not to worry, but—'

Xandros gave her what reassurance he could. 'Well, she has a mind of her own—she'll turn up when she wants to.'

It was the best he could say. No point giving voice to his own growing suspicions of just why Ariadne had bolted, or where she might be now… She was no longer his concern.

Only her half-sister was. The half-sister who held a sensual allure for him that Ariadne had never had, for all her dark beauty. The half-sister he was due to marry in a handful of days, as soon as the paperwork permitted.

His mother would not come—it would be easier that way, both for her and for his bride. After all, theirs was not going to be a *real* marriage—not by anything other than legal definition. It was simply a means to an end. Two ends. Business, yes. And also pleasure…

The low purring started up along with the powerful engine of his car as he headed back to Athens. Oh, yes…very, very decided pleasure. Pleasure that he was having to exercise all his self-control not to start indulging in before the knot was tied.

That tantalising but fleeting kiss in the hotel restaurant was a torment to remember, and when she'd come to see his apartment he'd had to busy himself with his mail in order to keep his hands off her. Especially when he'd found her gazing at his bed…as if she were already envisaging them there together.

He'd so very nearly obliged her… But he'd drawn back, permitting himself only that light, brief touch on her shoulders—and even that had been a torment before he'd released her again…

It was a torment he was schooling himself to endure.

A rushed seduction in a hotel room, or even at his apartment, was not what he wanted. No, there was only one place he wanted to make Rosalie his own…

One perfect place he yearned to be with her…

CHAPTER EIGHT

THEY WERE DINING out the night before their wedding. Not at the hotel this time, but at what was obviously a very exclusive restaurant. Rosalie was thankful that it wasn't crowded or noisy. Nor was it, as far as she could tell, a fashionable watering hole for their generation.

'I thought you might like somewhere quiet,' Xandros said as they sat down at their table. 'This place is one of my mother's favourites when she's in town, for that very reason.'

Rosalie looked at him. 'Your mother?' Her brow furrowed and she spoke hesitantly. 'I...I didn't realise that she was still...well, still alive.'

'Very much so,' Xandros answered drily. 'She doesn't live in Athens, but out in the country. I'll take you to meet her sometime after our wedding.' He paused, and then he said, quite deliberately, 'She understands about our marriage.'

He didn't say any more, and Rosalie didn't probe. After all, did it really matter if Xandros's mother existed? It wasn't as if she was going to be a *real* mother-in-law any more than Xandros was going to be a real husband. And not just because their marriage was going to be so brief...

Her eyes went to him as he consulted the waiter about tonight's menu choices, taking in, as she always did, the sable feathering of his hair, the curve of his sensual mouth, the dark, long-lashed expressive eyes. She felt her senses heighten, wanting only to gaze at him, at just how incredibly, fatally attractive he was…

She remembered how she'd gazed at him that very first time, open-mouthed, when she'd opened the door of that rundown rental property to see him, unable to tear her eyes away from him.

And she still couldn't.

The same feeling of regretful melancholy went through her as she'd felt in his apartment. She must learn to subdue her growing longings. She must accept that she had read too much into that brief, fleeting and unrepeated kiss of greeting at the hotel restaurant that first night. For him it had been nothing more than a casual public salutation. It had meant nothing more than that.

'Pre-wedding nerves?' he asked.

He'd caught her expression and misinterpreted it, and she was glad he had—because there was no point him thinking anything else.

'There truly is no need for them,' he said. His dark eyes held hers. 'Rosalie, I want you to enjoy the kind of life you've never had before.'

His eyes washed over her and she felt their force—impossible not to. Any woman would feel it. Especially one so starved of romance as she was…

But Xandros was making it clear that he didn't want romance to be a part of their marriage. So, although his eyes were warm upon her, although he always complimented her on her appearance, his attitude towards her was nothing more than friendly, easy-going and companionable.

She must be glad of that—grateful. Grateful that her of hardship and endless penny-pinching was done with. That, after all, was why she was marrying Xandros. For nothing more.

She must remember that.

Or else torment herself with yearning for what was not going to happen…

So stop mooning over him! Don't long for what he isn't interested in! Just match his own attitude towards you—it's all he wants.

And that was what she did determinedly as they dined—on yet another exquisite gourmet meal of the kind that was now her daily diet.

She would be grateful for that, too—every day—and never take it or anything else about this luxurious life she was living for granted!

Afterwards, he took her back to her hotel, insisting cheerfully that he would see her to her room.

The thickly carpeted corridor leading to Rosalie's room was hushed and quiet and deserted.

'You don't have to walk me to my room!' she protested good-humouredly. 'I won't get lost!'

'You might totter off down the wrong corridor on those towering high heels,' he replied at her mild protest.

She gave a light laugh, and acquiesced, yet she was conscious of the empty length of corridor stretching ahead of them and of being alone with Xandros. It made her ultra-aware of him…of his presence at her side. It would have been easier, she thought ruefully, to say goodnight in the lobby.

They reached her door and she fumbled in her bag for her key, nerves jangling out of nowhere. She turned, the key card in hand, ready to say a bright goodnight, but the word died on her lips.

He was standing close to her—too close—but she couldn't back away. The door was behind her. She was conscious—suddenly, burningly—not just of how close he was, but how she could catch the faint scent of his aftershave, see in the dim light of the empty corridor how his strong jaw was already faintly etched with re-growth, giving him a seductively raffish look in his dark lounge suit.

She felt a flush of heat go through her and was suddenly conscious, too, of how the dress she was wearing—a close-fitting, beautifully tailored cocktail dress—was moulding her body, her breasts and her hips. Conscious, above all, of how breathless she was…

He was smiling down at her—but not with the familiar, nothing more than friendly smile he usually gave her. This was a different smile. One she had seen only once before… That first evening they had dined together…

Her breath caught and she could do nothing at all except let his smile wash over her, his eyes holding hers even as she felt him take her key card from her nerveless fingers and slide it down the lock, pressing the door open with a splay of his hand.

That smile tugged at his mouth…his sensual, sculpted mouth.

'This time tomorrow,' he said, his voice low, 'we shall be married. And it will be fine, Rosalie, I promise you. It will bring us everything we want.'

She could only gaze at him, saying nothing at all.

She could hear her heart thudding in her chest and there was not a scrap of air in her lungs. Her eyes were widening…pupils dilating…

She saw something change in his eyes, intensify, and heard him say something in Greek…something that sounded rasping. Then he was speaking in English.

'You know…' he said softly.

And out of nowhere she felt the timbre in his voice doing things to her, sending her blood pulsing through her veins in a hot, hectic throb that she could not stop—could not stop at all.

'You really shouldn't look at me like that…'

'Like what…?'

The words were faint on her breath—the breath that was not in her lungs. That throbbing pulse was at her throat, at her temple, in the deep core of her body—the body that was now yearning infinitesimally towards him, her face lifted to his, gazing up at him with wide eyes.

And in his eyes she could see, in the dark, sweeping depths, a glint of pure gold. The tug at his mouth deepened, half-rueful, half-anticipatory.

'Like you want me to do…this…' he said.

And as he spoke, in that low, soft voice, she saw his lashes sweep down over his eyes, his face lower to hers.

His lips touched hers and his kiss was velvet silk, brushing slowly, seductively across her mouth, easing her own lips apart, softly and surely, deepening his slow, leisurely tasting of her until he was taking his fill…

Bliss went through her, pure and exquisite, and she gave her mouth to him, let him taste and take her, explore and possess…

She felt her body sway towards his, her eyes flutter shut as she gave herself to what was happening.

Xandros was kissing her…

Kissing her in a way that made that earlier, brief, fleeting kiss seem nothing more than the merest promise of what a kiss could be…

Kissing her as she had never thought it possible for a kiss to be!

And she was melting into it, drowning in it, this the softest, most sensuous sensation in the entire universe, this the exquisite honeyed feathering of his mouth on hers.

It seemed to go on and on, and she was weak with it, faint with it…

And she wanted more…oh, so much more…

A low, helpless moan sounded in her throat, and as if with an instinct of their own her hands reached around him to draw his body to hers, to feel the hard, strong column of his back beneath her fingers—

At her touch he pulled away from her in sharp withdrawal, his mouth releasing hers abruptly, his hand moving away from the door.

Her eyes flew open.

He was looking down at her with an expression that was closed—shuttered, even—and she gazed at him in a helpless haze, lips still parted…

She saw him take a breath. A ragged inhalation. Saw him take a step backwards.

He shook his head. 'This was a mistake,' he said.

There was a blankness in his voice, and he took another breath, deeper than the first, his expression changing again.

'It's late. You should get some sleep. I must go.' He reached past her to push her door open wider. 'Go in, Rosalie,' he said. His voice was firm and his mouth tightened. 'You need to get to bed. We have to be with the registrar by eleven.'

She felt his hand on the small of her back. Broad and impersonal. Turning her towards her room.

She caught the edge of the door, instinctively resisting. Trying to turn back to him.

'I…'

The pulse at her throat was throbbing, and there was a flush of heat across her cheeks. Her lips were still parted. Still yearning for his…

And as her eyes lifted to his she knew yearning filled them. A yearning she could not crush, or halt, or do anything about. For the blood was still beating in her veins, blinding her to everything but the kiss they had shared.

'No.'

There was harshness in his voice. Rejection.

'Rosalie—*goodnight*!'

He turned away, and then he was striding down the hushed and deserted corridor, his gait rapid, gaining the end in moments, turning towards the elevator, lost to her sight.

She felt emptiness, desolation, as she went into her room. He had kissed her in a way she had never known a kiss could be. A kiss to melt her to her very core. And then he had set her aside.

His rejection echoed in her head.

'This was a mistake.'

A cry broke from her.

* * *

Xandros stood out on his apartment's balcony, staring at the floodlit Acropolis, not seeing it. He was hearing his own words echo in his head.

'This was a mistake.'

His hands tightened over the railing. *Thee mou*, one hell of a mistake! It had taken all his strength to push her inside—keeping himself on the outside—and to turn and walk away, with every step wanting to turn around and stride back to her, to step inside her room and—

No! Don't go there! Not even in imagination! Least of all that...

He took a shuddering breath. He'd been a rash and reckless fool to walk her back to her room—he should have resisted the temptation. But he hadn't wanted to say goodnight quite yet. Had wanted to prolong the evening with her. Prolong it in a much more intimate way…

No! He was heading down dangerous paths again.

He clenched his jaw, exerting control over himself just as he had since that evening he'd allowed himself the sweet pleasure of greeting her with that all too brief and fleeting kiss. It had taught him that any contact with her would be like a match to tinder. That he must control himself, deny himself, until he had her all to himself.

As he would tomorrow.

Tomorrow night…the start of their honeymoon. The start of their marriage, when she would be his…

That low purring started up in him, so familiar to him now whenever he thought of the breathtakingly alluring woman who would soon—oh, so achingly soon now—be his entirely…

And until then…

He turned away, clicking shut the balcony doors and striding into his bedroom, stripping off his tie as he did so, slipping his cufflinks.

His eyes glinted. Until then the traditional remedy for thwarted passion was going to be very necessary.

He headed for the en-suite bathroom. Time for a cold shower. A *very* cold one…

Rosalie gazed, enthralled, as the helicopter started its descent, feeling again the leap of pleasure she'd felt when Xandros had announced, just after their wedding that morning, that he was taking her to his private island for their honeymoon.

She hadn't thought they would have a honeymoon at all—not in a marriage like theirs. But then she had realised that, just as he wanted her to wear the fabulous diamond engagement ring and also, since the simple brief ceremony that morning, which had passed in a blur of Greek with an English translation for herself in a room at the town hall, her new wedding ring, so a honeymoon would be expected as well. To show the world—show her father—that theirs was a proper marriage.

And she knew she could be glad that it was to be on Kallistris. On Xandros's private island they wouldn't be on view for anyone else to think it odd they weren't all loved-up…

Her eyes shadowed momentarily but she banished her thoughts. Last night had been…*difficult.* The understatement rang hollow. But in the sleepless hours that had followed she had come to terms with it. She'd had to.

Xandros had kissed her—she'd all but begged him to, and mortification burned in her as she remembered what he'd said to her—and promptly regretted it. Well, she had learnt her lesson. From now on she would be only what he wanted her to be—bright, cheerful, friendly, appreciative, enthusiastic…

She ran out of adjectives to describe the way she would need to be with this man who had called kissing her a mistake, and went back to gazing, rapt, as the little island—the smallest of a small cluster set in the azure Aegean—loomed closer and closer. And then they had landed, setting down on a small helipad by the sea's edge.

Xandros vaulted out, thanking the pilot, and Rosalie, glad she'd changed out of her tailored wedding outfit into cotton trousers and top at the hotel before setting off, jumped down lightly. Xandros, too, had changed out of his customary business suit into chinos and an open-necked shirt—looking just as drop-dead gorgeous as he always looked.

Rosalie sighed inwardly.

'Mind the downdraft!' he warned, and hurried her to the edge of the helipad as the helicopter took off again in a whirl of rotors.

As it disappeared, Xandros turned to her. 'Welcome to Kallistris,' he said.

His eyes were warm, his smile warmer. She felt her insides give a little skip, but she only smiled back, and then both of them turned as a Jeep came rattling along the coastal track towards them.

'Ah,' said Xandros, looking pleased. 'Panos.'

The weather-beaten face of his island's caretaker broke into a huge smile as Xandros introduced him, warning Rosalie that Panos spoke little English, but that his wife, Maria, was more fluent.

'Kalimera,' said Rosalie, gingerly trying out her highly limited Greek.

Her hand was taken in a bear grip, and shaken vigorously.

'Kyria Lakaris!' exclaimed Panos, and it gave Rosalie a start to hear her married name.

I'll have to get used to it, she thought to herself.

Just as she would have to get used to living with Xandros…but as friends, nothing more than that.

She dragged her eyes away from him, hoping forlornly that perhaps with time she would stop wanting to gaze endlessly at him, because now they were married she was going to have to inure herself to his constant presence. She swallowed.

They set off in the Jeep. Xandros chatted in Greek to Panos and Rosalie hung tightly to the window frame as they bumped rapidly along the unmetalled track.

They rounded a rocky promontory, and she gave an exclamation of spontaneous delight. 'Oh, how beautiful!'

They were looking down on to a small but perfectly formed bay, its furthest end bounded by another promontory. Between the two stretched a pristine pebbled beach lapped by the azure sea that girded the whole island. Nestled in the centre, just above the beach, was a small one-storey villa, framed by a mix of silvery olive trees and pink-flowered oleanders.

It was like something on a picture postcard, whitewashed, with a blue door and matching blue window shutters, the whole house festooned with vivid, crimson bougainvilleas.

'Do you like it?' Xandros turned to her.

'It's perfect!' she enthused.

She felt her mood lift. However difficult it was going to be to be here, alone with Xandros, having to conceal her hopeless susceptibility to him, surely the opportunity to be in this beautiful place would make it worthwhile! Never again in her life would she have a chance to holiday on a private Aegean island.

Xandros gave a slashing grin as Panos screeched to a halt in a cloud of white dust and helped her down as a stout, middle-aged woman bustled out through the blue door.

'Welcome, welcome!' Panos's wife greeted them, and then embraced Xandros in a bear hug, chattering away to him in Greek, before guiding Rosalie inside the little villa, saying, 'Come! Come!' in enthusiastic tones.

Inside it was much cooler, and Maria led the way off to the left, down a tiled corridor and into a room that was, Rosalie surmised, going to be her bedroom. Xandros's must be the one beyond.

Did Maria and Panos realise that she was not a true bride in any sense? What had Xandros told them about their marriage?

She gave a mental shrug—that was his concern, not hers.

Panos delivered her suitcase and Maria hefted it on to the bed to start unpacking. Rosalie moved to help, but was waved away.

'Go! Go to your husband!' Maria ordered her.

Giving in, Rosalie ventured out into the corridor, making her way outdoors. The heat of the afternoon hit her immediately, and the crystal-clear sea lapping the pebbled beach beckoned. She kicked off her sandals, turned up her trouser hems, then waded ankle-deep into the cool water.

'This is joyous!' she exclaimed.

Footsteps crunched on the pebbles behind her.

'I'm glad you think so.'

Xandros's voice sounded warm, and Rosalie turned. He'd swapped his chinos for denim shorts, his open-necked shirt for a pristine white tee, and Rosalie was instantly and vividly aware of how the tee moulded his muscled torso, how the denim cut-offs revealed his lithe and powerful bare legs.

She snapped her gaze away, looking instead at his face—which wasn't much help, for he was sporting aviator sunglasses. The breeze was lightly ruffling his dark hair, and he looked just ludicrously, jaw-droppingly attractive.

She gave a gulp.

Sexy—the overused word was impossible to dismiss. Impossible to deny. It described him totally. Even though it was a completely pointless way of describing him...given the nature of their marriage...

She gulped again, trying to sound normal as she answered. 'Who wouldn't?' she returned with a half-laugh. 'Everyone who comes here must think so!'

'No one comes here,' Xandros said.

Rosalie's expression altered and she looked at him, puzzled.

'This is my sanctuary,' Xandros was saying now. 'I don't bring anyone here.'

Except a wife who isn't a real wife on a honeymoon that isn't a real honeymoon...

The words hung in her head, unsaid. Impossible to say. Unnecessary.

He went on speaking, changing the subject, and she was glad.

'Maria's just serving some refreshments. You must be thirsty, I'm sure.'

She followed him up the beach into the welcome cool under a huge cantilevered parasol that shaded a table and chairs in front of the villa, where Maria was setting down a tray laden with coffee, fruit juice, water and a plate of syrupy nut-strewn pastries.

'Eat,' she instructed, and bustled off.

Rosalie gratefully poured herself a glass of juice, cut it with iced water, and knocked it back appreciatively.

'Are you going to mortally offend Maria and not eat one of her pastries?'

Xandros's laconic question interrupted her train of thought.

'They look delicious, but I've been eating like a pig since…well, since I was let loose on gourmet food!' Rosalie answered lightly. 'I'll be as fat as one too if I keep going the same way!'

Dark eyes washed over her assessingly. 'I think that unlikely.'

Xandros's voice was dry, and there was something about it that made her own mouth suddenly dry. She wished he hadn't looked at her the way he had.

He doesn't understand the impact he has—even just saying things like that.

The trouble was, it didn't help her that he didn't…

I have to make myself not react! I have to! Or I'll never survive this honeymoon, never mind six months of being married to him...

In her head she heard yet again the brief, stark words he'd said to her last night before he'd walked away.

'This was a mistake.'

Those were the words she had to remember.

The only words.

CHAPTER NINE

'So, DO YOU fancy a swim?' Xandros pushed his empty coffee cup aside, drained his iced water and looked across at Rosalie. His breath caught silently. In formal daywear and nightwear she looked breathtaking, but in casual gear she looked every bit as stunning…

He got to his feet. A swim would be good for more than just cooling off and freshening up. It would take his mind off what he would like to do right now. Sweep her off her feet and into his bedroom—his bed.

But she wasn't ready for that yet, and he was no clumsy teen, wanting to rush his fences. Their wedding night would come—but not now.

'How about it?' he asked, looking down at her.

She smiled and stood up. 'Sounds wonderful,' she said. 'I'll go and get changed.'

He did likewise, and five minutes later was at the water's edge. He watched her come out of the villa, in a one-piece swimsuit covered in a beach wrap, her hair pinned up on top of her head. His breath caught again—she looked so lovely…

She also looked self-conscious, and with a gallantry he hadn't known he possessed he gave her a half-wave, then waded into the water, executing a duck dive and surfacing into a powerful freestyle, heading out to sea.

Far enough out, he turned, treading water. She'd discarded her wrap and was knee-high in the water. 'Come on in! It's not cold!' he called to her.

'It's gorgeous!' she called back, and went on wading in, to chest height.

Then, lifting her arms, she plunged into a breaststroke and headed out towards him. When she was near she halted, rolling on to her back, slowly extending her legs and arms to keep herself afloat, closing her eyes against the brightness of the sun.

Xandros watched her offering her fabulous body to the sun, with nothing but the material of the turquoise one-piece between it and her nakedness…

Something quickened inside him and moved—something he had not felt before—as she floated, so still…so achingly beautiful.

His gaze feasted upon her.

I could kiss her now, as she floats on the water, eyes closed, lips parted...

Almost he succumbed to the temptation welling up in him. But wiser counsel prevailed. They were out of their depth at this distance, and any kind of kiss would soon find them both under the surface and flailing for air. No, there would be time enough for kisses. Kisses and so much more…

'You look like a basking mermaid,' he said instead, a smile in his voice.

She did not open her eyes. 'I feel like one,' she answered. 'This is absolute bliss.'

He turned on his back and floated wide himself. 'It is,' he confirmed.

He went on floating beside her peacefully for a while, bobbing in the gentle swell, keeping his eyes shut against the bright sunshine. He was conscious that they were drifting further out to sea. He said as much to Rosalie, turning himself over to check their distance from the shore. She did likewise.

'But the Mediterranean is tideless, isn't it?' she asked.

'There's a slight tide—and definitely currents—but nothing like what you're used to in Britain,' he answered, and they both started to make their way with a slow breaststroke back towards the beach.

'I'm not used to the seaside anywhere,' she replied. 'I've never been till now.'

Xandros's expression changed. 'You've *never* been to the seaside?' His voice was disbelieving.

'Not even Southend!' she exclaimed, half-humorously, half-sadly. 'That's the closest seaside for East Enders, but Mum was never well enough to go. Never well enough for anything, really—not that there was any money for holidays anyway,' she finished.

Now he could hear more sadness in her voice than humour. Pity for her filled him, and resolve, too—to do whatever he could to compensate her for the deprivations of her impoverished life. Even in the darkest days of his childhood, when money worries for his parents had been at their height, he had enjoyed an affluence way beyond Rosalie's.

Well, now she would enjoy not only mere affluence, but luxury—all that he could provide for her. Every luxury—and every pleasure.

He felt his brow furrowing as he swam. It was new to him to entertain such an impulse. All the women he'd been involved with had come from his own world, used to luxury and expensive living—Ariadne included. And for none of them—not even Ariadne—had he felt this overwhelming desire to provide for them. Make them happy.

His eyes went to her now as she swam beside him, her gaze focussed on the approaching beach.

I want to make her happy! That's exactly what I want to do!

It was a strange feeling. A novel feeling. A good feeling.

And it was a feeling he went on feeling, bringing to him an inner warm glow as they waded ashore.

'If you've any energy left, let's go for a walk. I'll show you something of the island. Nothing too strenuous, I promise.'

Nor was it.

Showered and dressed again, he led the way up a narrow path through the thickly growing oleander bushes on the far side of the beach.

As they reached the clifftop, and the vista of the rugged coastline and the wild, maquis-covered terrain opened up before them, Rosalie gave a smile of pleasure at his side.

'Oh, it's beautiful!' she said enthusiastically.

Xandros looked at her, smiling himself. She was wearing sunglasses, and her hair was caught back with a barrette. But it was being winnowed by the wind spilling off the clifftop. She pushed it back with her hand, taking in the view. Her beauty was natural, unforced. He wanted to do nothing but gaze at her and drink it in.

Then, abruptly, she started. A goat, followed by

several more, leapt from behind some low bushes, disturbed by their presence, bounding away inland.

'They're supposed to be feral,' Xandros told her, 'But Maria feeds them if she thinks they look hungry. In exchange, she milks them and makes cheese. I expect we'll sample some tonight at dinner. Speaking of which,' he went on, 'we'd better head back. We'll come up another day—bring a picnic lunch with us. It's a great spot for watching the sunset, too—though tonight it's going to be the Champagne Sunset Show, down on the beach.'

She smiled. 'Sounds good,' she answered.

'And we must brace ourselves,' he said, humour in his voice, 'for Maria will have excelled herself with dinner. She's been cooking all day, Panos told me.'

A wedding feast. A wedding feast to fill them both up. Give them energy for the night ahead.

Their wedding night…

Rosalie glanced at her reflection in the long mirror on the wall in her bedroom. Her brushed cotton dress fell in soft butter-yellow folds to her ankles from a high waistline. The slight bodice was ruched over her breasts, skimming her shoulders. She'd draped a creamy embroidered shawl around her, held her hair back with a narrow headband. Her make-up was minimal—some mascara and lip gloss—and her fragrance was a light floral scent, not the heavier perfume she had indulged in in Athens.

She frowned uncertainly. Though she wasn't in the least glitzed up, as she had been in Athens, should she have dressed up at all? Would Xandros think she was trying to send a message he did not wish to hear, as he had made so clear last night?

Well, her behaviour towards him must show him otherwise, that was all. She had managed it so far—that walk up to the clifftop had gone okay, and all she had to do was keep that going. Be interested in what he said, be cheerful and friendly and easy-going.

And not look at him too often…

She made her way outside to the beach, to find Xandros already there, relaxing back in a canvas chair, long legs outstretched. The sun was low on the horizon, bathing the scene in rich red gold.

'Come and sit down.' He got to his feet. 'The sunset show is about to begin.'

There was an ice bucket on a table, and in it an open bottle of champagne. Rosalie took her seat and Xandros resumed his, pouring a flute for each of them.

She took hers from him, conscious of the slight brush of his fingers as she did so. Now, in profile against the lowering sun, she saw his eyes resting on her. Saw the warm glow on her.

'To our marriage,' he said, and lifted his glass to tilt it against hers. 'May it bring everything to us that we want.'

It was something she could drink to, and did, but even as she did so she was conscious of the tug of that strange melancholy again.

But what if I want more from it than you do?

It was a dangerous thought, and a useless thought, for she knew perfectly well why they had married and what it would give them. A great deal.

But not each other.

That was not what their marriage was about and she

must remember it. Remember it with piercing purpose now, as she took a sip of the beautifully beading liquid, felt its bouquet shimmer in her mouth.

For a moment—just a moment—their eyes met over the flutes and she felt something shimmer deep inside her along with the champagne's bouquet…

She turned her head away, lest her eyes reveal it. Gazed out over the water, shading from azure to gold as the sun lowered. Neither talked, as if by mutual consent, just watched quietly, the only sound that of the wavelets lapping onto the pebbles.

Moment by moment the sun pooled into the waiting Aegean.

And was gone.

Xandros pushed back his chair, getting to his feet. 'I can smell the fruits of Maria's labours. It would not do to be late for them!'

They strolled back to the villa, Xandros taking the champagne with him, and made their way round to the gable end of the house, beyond their bedrooms. There was a pretty little stone-flagged terrace, girded by a low wall on which sat pots of red and white geraniums. A vine-covered pergola arched over it, threaded with fairy-lights which also wound around the wooden supports of the pergola.

A table was set with a white linen tablecloth, a centrepiece of fragrant white flowers and a huge candle in a glass holder which gave a soft glow to the whole scene. Rosalie's face broke into a rapturous smile. It was all so enchantingly beautiful.

She exclaimed and said as much, and Xandros smiled, ushering her to the table, refilling their champagne flutes.

Then Maria was bustling out to the terrace, emerging from somewhere at the back of the villa where, Rosalie presumed, the kitchen was situated.

'Welcome! Welcome!' She beamed. Then, 'Eat, eat!' she instructed, depositing upon the table a vast platter groaning with food.

Mounds of delicious-smelling slices of slow-cooked lamb were layered over fragrant rice and roasted potatoes, lapped with green beans and fried tomatoes… There was enough to feed way more than just themselves.

'I did warn you,' Xandros said, catching Rosalie's eye, his mouth tugging in a smile.

'Where are the dozen other dinner guests?' she responded humorously.

He laughed, and began to serve up.

Rosalie gave a moan of appreciation. It all tasted incredible. The herb-crusted lamb melted in her mouth—it had been slow roasting over charcoal for hours, Xandros told her—and the accompaniments, hearty as they were, tasted, to her mind, better than all the gourmet food she'd been revelling in since Xandros had lifted her of the poverty she'd known all her life.

'This is so *good*!' she enthused.

Maria emerged yet again, this time bringing an open bottle of red wine, depositing that, too, on the table with a flourish.

Rosalie ventured another line of phrasebook Greek, trying to saying how good the food was, and acquired a volley of approving speech in return.

Xandros translated for her. 'She says you need to be strong for your wedding night,' he told her.

In the candlelight there was a knowing glint in his

eyes that Rosalie found difficult to cope with. But then reason came to the rescue.

He knows the irony of that. That's what that glint is for.

A shadow fluttered over her and she reached for her flute again, to banish it. But as the meal progressed it was hard to keep to her resolve not to be beguiled by everything about Xandros.

He'd always been attentive to her when they'd dined together in Athens, but this evening, under the fairy-lights woven into the vines, in the soft, flickering candlelight, she could see his eyes constantly on her. Warm…glinting…

She tried to ward it off.

He doesn't realise the effect he's having! That's the thing—he doesn't mean it...doesn't intend it. It just comes naturally to him. It's part of who he is.

The most intensely attractive male she could imagine, let alone have set eyes on in real life.

She fought it—she had to—but it was getting harder by the minute.

He'd poured a full glass of red wine for her, and its heady strength could not be denied. Perhaps it was not wise of her to imbibe so freely, but it washed the rich lamb down so perfectly it was hard to refrain.

Her plate was empty now, finally, but then there was a smaller second helping for them both, because it was so good it was impossible to refrain from that.

But when Maria re-emerged, whisking away the remnants and then replacing the lamb with another platter groaning with pastries, Rosalie gave an echoing groan.

She sat back, shaking her head. 'I couldn't! Not a thing!'

Across the table from her, Xandros laughed, picking up his wine glass and draining it. 'These are different from this afternoon. Lighter. Filled with curd cheese and honey. Try one. You'll like it, I promise you.'

Tempted, she did just that, and he was right—it was delicious.

'Is this the goat's cheese you told me about?' she asked Xandros brightly. That was better, surely? Asking about goats and cheese…anything that wasn't about the way his dark, long-lashed eyes were resting on her…

He nodded, helping himself to several of the pastries and starting to demolish them. Where they all went, Rosalie wasn't sure—certainly not into body fat.

Memory leapt in her—seeing him stripped down to swim shorts had been even more disturbing than seeing him when he'd been wearing that moulding white tee. In the sea she'd been able to see what it had been moulding. A perfectly honed torso, with smooth, golden pecs, and ripped and rippling abs…

She banished the memory. Definitely not a safe one. Not when she had a glass of champagne and nearly two of red wine inside her.

A sense of danger caught at her. She must not succumb—*must not!*—to the seductive aura all around her. Xandros opposite her, the gold-flecked glint of his eyes resting on her, lounging back, looking so lithe, so fabulous, so incredibly tempting…

I have to resist it! Resist him! Resist everything about him—everything he does to me when I'm gazing at him like this...

Because he didn't want her—not in that way.

Into her head came the words he'd thrown at her last night as he'd broken away from their kiss.

'This was a mistake.'

And it *would* be a mistake—*her* mistake this time!—for her to carry on indulging in gazing at him the way she wanted to. Indulging herself in anything about him at all. What did she know of men? Her romance-starved, constricted life had given her no experience—let alone of a man like Xandros.

He'd finished his pastries and was pushing his empty plate away from him, his gaze resting on her with half-closed eyes. She tried to drop her own gaze because she knew she should...must...but found she couldn't. She tried not to be aware of how she could feel her pulse beating at her throat—but she couldn't ignore it. It was impossible...just impossible.

He leaned forward suddenly, reaching out with his napkin in his hand. 'You've got a pastry crumb caught on your lip,' he said.

His voice was husky as he dabbed at the offending particle, his fingers just brushing the soft curve of her mouth.

She felt the pulse at her throat surge, her breath go still in her lungs. Her eyes held his, helpless to do anything else.

The candle was burning low in its glass case, starting to gutter, and the heady scent of the white flowers in the centrepiece—jasmine, Xandros had told her earlier, when she'd asked—caught at her senses.

He caught at her senses.

Xandros—the man she had married. Married that morning, making her his wife. A wife who was not a wife—not the way real wives were—for that was not why they had married. Not to sit here with him at this candlelit table, under fairy-lights that echoed the stars blazing in the heavens far above them, while soft waves lapped on the beach and a choir of cicadas chorused in the unseen vegetation beyond the little terrace. Not to see the eyes of the man she had married that morning resting on her with a gaze that was turning her slowly and unstoppably into liquid mush…

He was getting to his feet. She heard the scrape of his chair on the stone paving, and then he was beside her.

'Shall we skip coffee?' he said.

He was smiling down at her, a half-smile through half-closed eyes that were resting on her upturned face. The smile deepened, curving the edges of his mouth—his perfect, sculpted mouth—indenting lines around it that shadowed the planes of his face in the soft, low light. His eyes washed over her again, and in their depths she could see that dark gold seductive glint again. No hint of irony in it now…

She felt the breath leave her body.

'There's an age-old custom I want to try out,' he said, and his voice was husky again.

She didn't see it coming—was incapable of doing so. She could only give a breathless gasp as he scooped her bodily into his arms, striding with her into the villa.

He gave a laugh of triumph and possession. 'Carrying my bride over the threshold!'

She could say nothing, do nothing, could only gasp again, her arm automatically hooking around his neck, feeling the strength of his shoulders, feeling her body cradled against his.

'Xandros!' she cried out, half in consternation, half in bewilderment.

She was utterly overcome.

Overcome by being in his arms, lifted by him, her body caught against his strong muscled torso, his grip encompassing her totally.

He strode along the short length of the corridor, swept her into a bedroom.

Not hers, but his.

He laid her down upon his bed, flicked on the bed-side light, came down beside her. Propped himself up to gaze down at her.

She could not breathe…could not speak. Blood was drumming in her veins, her eyes, and she could only stare up at him, gaze helplessly. His eyes were pouring into hers, and now they were not half closed at all, but blazing with a gold that was not a glint but a molten pool.

'I have been waiting for this moment all day,' he said, and there was a rasp in his voice. '*All day.* Waiting…' He took a ragged breath. 'Waiting since I saw you sashay out of that restaurant in London before we flew out to Athens. And now, finally, my wait is over.'

His head lowered, his mouth dipping to hers. And she was lost. Lost utterly in a bliss she could not stop because it was him kissing her. Xandros kissing her with a slow, feathered touch that was deepening all the time, parting her lips, reaching within, purposeful, tasting, seeking…finding. Melding.

It was a kiss as devastating to her as the kiss he had given her last night at her hotel room doorway. A hundred times more devastating! A thousand—

She could not stop him. Did not want to. Wanted only to let her eyes flutter shut and give herself to the exquisite feathering of his lips on hers, the soft, persuasive caress of his mouth as he eased hers open, deepening the kiss.

Bliss took over—sheer, gorgeous, unalloyed, insistent bliss. Bliss that went on and on as his hands tightened on her, as his mouth drew from hers yet more response.

A sense of sweeping oblivion overcame her as everything, in the entire universe ceased to exist except this moment, now, this moment that went on and on.

Until, as if he were pulling away under the strongest duress, he lifted his mouth from hers. His gaze was a wash of desire that blazed from him like the sun.

'Welcome to our wedding night,' he said.

CHAPTER TEN

ROSALIE STILLED, HIS words echoed, lifting her from the pool of sensual oblivion in which she had been drowning with his kiss.

Confusion filled her. 'I…I don't understand.' The words fell from her, summing up the whirlpool of confusion inside her.

How could this be happening—*how*?

Xandros's brow furrowed as he drew back from her a little. 'Don't understand what?'

Then his brow cleared, a smile starting to play about his mouth, and she could see even in the dim lamplight those deep flecks of gold in his eyes that somehow made her feel breathless all over again.

'Isn't it very simple?' he asked.

'But…' She swallowed. 'You said it was a mistake. Last night… That kiss… At my room in the hotel—'

He stared down at her. Then a wry, rueful laugh broke from him. 'Do you have *any* idea how hard it was for me to walk away from your room last night?' he asked, and she could hear the husk beneath the rueful tone. '*That* was why kissing you was a mistake!'

He took a ragged breath.

'Do you have *any* idea how hard it has been to keep

my hands off you this entire time? That first evening at the hotel…at least we were in public—but when you came to my apartment, looked into my bedroom at my bed…'

Greek words broke from him, and then he was back to English.

'I've been in torment! Waiting to have you here all to myself…'

She gazed up at him, taking in his words. Taking in the implication of them. Something was soaring in her, taking flight, lifting her up and up and up…

'But now… Ah, now…' he went on, and his voice was husky again, with a sensual twist to it that set in motion inside her a vibration that seemed to be in every cell of her body. 'Now the time is right. Now,' he said, 'the time is perfect…'

He brushed his lips to hers again, softly, fleetingly. Arousingly. She gave herself to it, gave herself to *him*, to all that he was drawing from her, arousing in her—to the sense of wonder filling her, the wonderful, wondrous release of all that she had been trying so hard to keep in check, to stamp out of herself…

And now—like a fantasy made real, a dream come true—she did not have to! Because she had been so wrong about him! The truth was wonderful, glorious, like the blaze of desire that she could see in his eyes, pouring into hers now as his mouth lifted from her.

He wants me! He wants me as I have come to want him! And he can have everything he wants of me—everything...

She could feel her heart start to slug in slow, heavy beats, a throbbing deep inside her. Her senses were dizzy, hyperaware and yet dazed and dreamlike. The wine sang in her blood, but she was not intoxicated… not by wine.

He kissed her again, and now she was kissing him back, opening her mouth to his, letting him feast upon her as she did on him. She was taking his mouth with hers and then his mouth was lifting from hers again. And as he gazed down at her his dark eyes were pools of sensual desire that sent a thrill through her, a heady quickening of her pulse that was like nothing she had ever felt or known in all her life.

His hand was moving along her hair like a soft caress, the tips of his fingers touching her cheek, drawing along the contour of her cheekbone, tracing her jaw, lingering over her mouth, shaping it with his touch. His eyes poured over her and she could see those gold flecks, the lush, smoky lashes dipping down as he explored her parting lips yet again with his delicate, sensual touch.

His fingers trailed own the exposed column of her throat, slowly, deliberately. Oh, it was so achingly arousing. She could only gaze up at him, feeling every sense come vividly alive, twisting her fingers to catch at the soft pillow beneath her head.

His hand smoothed lower and her breath caught. Though he said not a word she knew what he intended—oh, she knew with an ache inside her…

'So very, very beautiful…'

The husk in his voice was a rasp now, and as he murmured the words his hand rounded over the sweet swell of her breast. Beneath his palm, through the thin material of her dress, the lacy fabric of her bra, her breast engorged, its peak flowering at his enfolding touch.

A groan broke from her, soft and low, and he gave an answering laugh, moving his mouth to take the place of his moulding palm. Another groan broke from her at this renewed and oh, so exquisitely delicious onslaught on her body. And even as his lips teased her through the thin fabric of her garments his hand was sliding the strap of the dress from her shoulder, taking with it her bra strap as well.

She was hardly conscious of it, her whole focus only on the sensations he was arousing in her with his sensuous ministrations to her peaking breast. Only when his hand cupped her did she realise, with a startled little intake of breath, that her breast was now exposed to his view—and to his touch.

Oh, his touch…!

Wonder filled her, and a sense of amazement, and along with that a growing, irresistible sense of arousal, of a sensual sexual excitement that was firing within her like a slow-burning flame that suffused her whole body, making a sudden restlessness fill her, so that every nerve ending seemed hyper-aroused and she was ultra aware of her own body…ultra aware of a growing, insistent need…a need for the blissful, arousing touch of his hands, his mouth, to intensify, to be everywhere, to stroke and caress and explore…

She felt her spine arching of its own accord, as if her body were inviting more of what his mouth and hand were doing at her breast. Another groan broke from her, in a kind of helpless surrender to what was happening to her—a surrender she was making with her own desire…

For a new hunger was building in her now—a new need not just to lie there, her hands flexing in the pillow, her eyes fluttering shut at the exquisite sensations his ministrations to her bared, exposed and achingly cresting breasts. He had bared both now to his touch and his mouth, and his lips were laving her peaked nipple, his sensitive fingers skilfully squeezing and scissoring.

This new hunger was moving her limbs restlessly, searchingly, and her seeking hand soon found what it wanted, snaking around the strong column of his neck, her fingers playing in his hair, while her other hand girdled the lean circuit of his waist, as if of its own volition pushing the material of his shirt free from his waistband, sliding across the warm, strong contours of his back.

It felt glorious, wonderful, exhilarating! And then her legs were sliding sideways, for suddenly she was aching to feel the full length of his body on hers, wanting to feel his hips against hers, his thighs lying within the cradle of hers, to feel—with shock, and amazement, and a catching of her breath in realisation—just what the full weight of his body on hers entailed…

Did he hear the revealing catching of her breath? He must have, for his mouth lifted from her breast and his eyes were pouring into hers now, those gold flecks burning to molten flame.

'Do you not know how much I desire you?' There was humour in his voice, but promise, too… His long eyelashes dipped over his molten gaze and his mouth lowered to hers. 'How very, very much…'

And suddenly the tenor of his embrace changed. Its slow sensuality quickened, and it was with an abrupt movement that he was pulling his shirt over his head, not bothering with anything so delaying as buttons, before coming down on her again, kissing her again, warmly, persuasively, ardently.

Then, briskly, he had rolled her over on to her front and was smoothing the material of her dress upwards, lifting her hips and waist, ridding her of all that was not necessary as he turned her back to face him, her long hair tangling around her throat, cascading over her naked breasts.

For a moment, endless and timeless, he gazed down at her. She heard Greek words breaking from him, and then English, as his gaze devoured her.

'You are so beautiful. Perfect…'

Then, with another sudden movement he stood up.

'Don't move.'

His voice was a growl, and in the dim light he towered over her, his golden torso bronze in the light from the lamps as she gazed upon the perfection she had known that baring would reveal to her.

And not just the perfection of his torso.

With a widening of her eyes she realised why he had stood up, for with brisk haste he was casting aside his chinos and the last remaining barrier between them…

She shut her eyes. It was instinctive, immediate, and even as she did it she heard him laugh. As if in triumph and satisfaction.

And then she felt his weight beside her on the bed, lying beside her. Felt his hand smooth her hair from her face as she dared to open her eyes again.

His gaze was pouring down on her once more, desire blazing…

Then his mouth lowering to hers again. And with bemused wonder she gave herself to every exquisite, sensual caress—for what did she know of how a couple made love, except what she had read or fantasised about in the long, lonely, empty years of her youth?

And now it was happening. Desire and growing passion were sweeping her away, unleashed kiss by kiss, touch by touch, caress by caress. Caresses that now, emboldened, she was seeking for herself, revelling in the muscled sinews and the warmth of his smooth skin, the contours and sculpting of his spine and hips and broad shoulders as an instinct as old as time urged her on.

Her spine arched, her breasts pressed against the wall of his chest and her hips crushed his. And then came the shock, the wonder of his arousal for her, his blatant desire, and, oh, the quickening of her own flesh, so that the hunger within her was growing, and mounting.

She wanted him—dear God, she wanted him… She wanted all of him, wanted his complete possession, wanted to give herself to him as a woman gave herself to a man…totally and all-consuming…

Her urgency and her hunger were his, answering his. He was cupping her shoulders, rearing up over her only to swoop down on her mouth with one last arousing full-throated kiss…and then he was plunging deep, deep within her as her thighs parted to receive him and her body opened to him…

Pain knifed through her and a piercing cry was torn from her throat. Her body froze.

Greek broke from him. Disbelief was in his eyes as he pulled away from her, staring down at her.

She could not move—could only feel the pain echoing still in her body…the body that was instinctively closing against him now. As it did so he was immediately freeing her, rolling sideways, lifting his weight from her.

His head whipped towards her and there was still that stunned disbelief in his face. 'Rosalie! *Thee mou*—why did you not *tell* me?'

Her body had curled instinctively into a foetal position, her thighs pressed close together, her arms, without his body to hold, fallen slackly to her sides.

She turned her head to him, her expression working, her body and her head a tumult. 'I…I…'

She could get no further. And suddenly, out of nowhere—out of the mountainous tower of her emotions and the overwhelming confusion of her mind and body over all that had swept over her—another tearing cry broke from her and she burst into tears. Tears for all that had happened…that had *not* happened.

Immediately, with an oath, he brought his arms around her—arms that held her, drew her towards him, rocked her in his embrace, cradling her like a child.

His voice was no longer shocked, but concerned—comforting. Cherishing. He spoke to her in Greek, soft and mellifluous, and she couldn't understand a word, nor hear it properly either, through the muffled sobs she stifled on his chest as her face pressed against it, her shoulders convulsing with her tears, her body shaking.

How long she wept, she didn't know, but she felt the tears easing from her, felt a kind of washed-out, exhausted calm overcoming her. And still he talked to her, softly and gently, his hand smoothing her back, comforting and reassuring her, holding her close and closer still against him as her body ceased its shaking, started to slacken in his arms.

Exhaustion washed over her, thickening the air, her breath. Her tear-filled eyes were stinging, her eyelids drooping. Her eyes were heavy, so very heavy…her breathing was slowing, easing…

And then sleep—sweet, sweet sleep—folded over her.

Xandros stood by the sea's edge, where the morning sun was bright on the water, his thoughts on the woman he had left sleeping in his bed—and not just any woman, not just one of his amours.

My wife. My bride. My virgin bride...

He felt his breath catch, felt the contours of his life changing, reshaping themselves. It felt strange. And strangely wonderful…

Footsteps crunching on the pebbled beach behind him made him turn. His face lit with a warm smile.

'Kalimera,' he said softly.

But his new wife—his bride—did not return his smile. Instead she paused in her hesitant approach towards him. He went to her, took her hands in his. She had put on a pair of turquoise shorts, a pink tee. Her hair was loose, she wore not a scrap of make-up—and she looked the most beautiful he had ever seen her…

He felt something turn over inside him.

But her expression was troubled.

He pressed her hands with his, compunction filling him. 'How are you?' he asked, with concern in his voice. 'I am so, so sorry if I… If I hurt you last night. But…' he took a rueful breath '…I simply didn't realise…'

He saw colour fill her cheeks, flushing them, watched her gaze drop. Compunction smote him again. He drew her closer to him, dropped a kiss as light as a feather upon her forehead. Her eyes flew up to his again. Their expression was still troubled.

'It's *me* who should be apologising!' The words broke from her. 'For…for disappointing you!'

Xandros could only stare at her. Could she really mean that? He kissed her again, on the mouth this time, swiftly, but without passion—only with reassurance.

'*Never* think that,' he said firmly His eyes held hers, intent with meaning. 'Never. From now on we will take things at the pace *you* set. And when the time is right—when you are ready—then everything will be all right.' He smiled down at her, his expression warm, his voice husky as he spoke. 'I promise you, my beautiful virgin bride, that when you cry out in my arms again it will only be from ecstasy…'

For a moment that was timeless, endless, his eyes held hers, infusing that promise deep into her. Then, knowing he had said enough for now—knowing, too, that if he held her this close any longer he would not be able to resist kissing her with passion—he gave her hands one last squeeze and let them go. He knew with every male instinct in him that a passionate kiss was not, alas, something she could cope with right now.

In quite a different voice, light and cheerful, he said, 'Time for breakfast. And today,' he added, 'we will simply—enjoy!'

Rosalie sat herself down at the table set at the front of the little villa. Maria bustled out with a tray piled high with breakfast.

'As ever, enough for half a dozen,' Xandros murmured good-humouredly as Maria disappeared again.

Rosalie gave a flickering smile. Xandros was being so *nice*—as cheerful and easy-going as he had been yesterday. Gratefully, she went with it. A sense of emotional exhaustion over anything else had taken her over, as if she just couldn't cope with anything else right now.

Besides, the scent of new-baked bread and the rich aroma of freshly brewed coffee plucked at her senses.

'Tuck in,' Xandros urged with a wide smile, passing her the butter and a pot of golden honey.

She felt her anxious thoughts ease a fraction. He was showing her a way to cope with them, to cope with the tumult of feelings inside her. And she would follow the lead he was setting for her, would find her own way, her own path. Take her time. She would feel only the ease of being here, in this beautiful place, and enjoy all it brought.

She would enjoy her breakfast, enjoy the loveliness of this beautiful island, and enjoy the sheer pleasure of eating *al fresco* like this, with the sun sparkling on the azure sea.

It was so infinitely distant from the life she had known till now, from the mean streets and ugliness of London—even from the busy bustle of Athens. This, here, now, was peace—absolute peace. Absolute beauty.

And Xandros was smiling at her—there was warmth in his voice, in his eyes… He was being so kind, so considerate.

Memory plucked at her of how kind he'd been that dreadful morning when she'd fled her father's house with all her stupid hopes smashed to pieces, when she'd sobbed all over Xandros… She'd done the same last night and he'd been just as kind…

She felt her heart swell and emotions swirled in her

again. Quite what they were, she did not know—she knew only that it was Xandros at their centre… Only Xandros.

'So, what would you like to do today?' he was asking now.

He was giving her, she knew with a little pang, a timely interruption to her thoughts…to emotions she could not yet make sense of.

'We could take a dip in the sea again, and then catch some rays before the sun gets too high. And then maybe, if you feel up to it, we could take the dinghy out later? How does that sound?'

She gave a flickering smile again, nodded. Letting him take the lead, guide her forward.

He wanted her to enjoy the day and she found that she did. It would have been impossible not to.

She swam, the cool salt water easing her body and the low ache between her legs dissipating, and then she let the sun warm her, giving herself to its golden balm. Then there was a leisurely *al fresco* lunch—more fresh bread, Maria's goat's cheese, sweet tomatoes and succulent home-grown olives. And afterwards, as he had promised, Xandros took her out on his dinghy, skimming them peacefully across the sun-drenched bay, back and forth, not talking while she leaned back, feeling the breeze fill her hair as well as the sail. Feeling a sense of peace fill her.

On their return, Maria attempted to feed them again, but Xandros took her for a walk—not up the cliffs this time, but inland, to Maria and Panos's home.

Panos proudly showed her his vegetable garden, groaning with produce, and his fruit-laden peach and lemon trees, and his olive grove, and his well-fed chickens and his stout pigs, and his two very fine-looking mules. She admired all of them unstintingly, and then he sat them down and plied them with almond biscuits washed down with a glass of his lethal home-distilled peach brandy, while his two deceptively fierce-looking dogs leaned heavily against Rosalie's legs, panting gently in the heat and inviting her to pet them, which she smilingly did.

Before they left Panos pressed a huge watermelon into Xandros's hands, and a basket of sun-warmed tomatoes into Rosalie's.

'Epharisto poli...nostimo!' she ventured, trying out her phrasebook Greek. She thought it meant 'Thank you...delicious!'

Panos's weathered face split into a huge grin, and with some voluble Greek he promptly added a pair of ripe peaches to the basket.

'We must make our getaway before we empty their larder!' Xandros murmured with a laugh, and they did just that.

They set off back to the villa, accompanied by Panos's dogs until he called them with a piercing whistle, whereupon they padded back to him.

'They have a good life, Panos and Maria,' Rosalie heard herself say. 'Simple, but good.'

'They do.' Xandros nodded. 'But you know...' his tone was thoughtful '...I sometimes wonder whether, if I tried to live like Maria and Panos, Kallistris would lose its magic. Sometimes when you have too much of something you enjoy, it palls.'

She glanced out to sea, thinking about what he'd said.

But I've had so little all my life! So little of anything, really—except my mother's love. In that, I have been rich indeed.

But of everything else she'd had so little as she'd grown up—even in comparison with her contemporaries. They had had girlfriends, boyfriends, romance in their lives…

Her eyes flickered back to the man walking along beside her, who could melt her with a single glance, a single touch, a single kiss. Who had revealed to her, last night, a desire that had swept her away into a sea of searing passion…until her inexperienced body had confused and confounded her.

But now he was promising her not shock and tears, but ecstasy in his arms…promising to make her truly his as she had never thought she would be.

He will be my lover—and I his...

She had not thought this strange, brief marriage would bring her that—had not looked for it or allowed herself to dream of it—but if it did, why be shy of it? Why refuse what she had never thought would be hers?

He wants me as I want him!

And why should that not be something to rejoice in? Even for the short duration of their time together? Her life had changed utterly in so short a time, all thanks to Xandros. She would be grateful to him for ever. Grateful for all he was making possible. Grateful that he desired her as she did him.

And it will be good—oh, so good! For he is everything I could ever dream about in a man! Everything!

The wonder of it filled her. She felt a warm rush around her heart and lifted her eyes to his. He caught them, smiling down at her, warm and caring.

For her and her alone.

For the night to come—when she would give herself to him and take all that he was offering her.

For all their time together.

In the dark of the night, in the warmth of his bed, she lay in his arms, filled with a golden incandescent glow. How was it possible to have felt such bliss, to have responded to his skilled, but oh, so gentle possession?

She had cried out—not in pain this time, but in wonder, just as he had promised her—and joy had flooded through her, along with a pleasure, an ecstasy so intense her spine had arched like a bow, her limbs straining, her hands clutching at the strong, straining sinews of his back. And he had thrown his head back as he, too, had reached that same peak of absolute union.

And now she lay in his arms, with an exhaustion so profound and a wonder so deep binding her to him as her hectic heart rate eased. She felt her breath, warm upon his strong, supporting chest, felt her eyelids close, sleep washing over her in the cradle of his arms.

In all the world this was the only place she wanted to be.

As he felt the soft, trembling body in his arms lapse into restful slumber Xandros slackened his hold. His own body was succumbing to the torpor of satiation, but before the last of his conscious thoughts ebbed from him he knew that one was uppermost. The one he treasured most.

Just as he had promised her he would, he had made it wonderful for her… And for himself as well.

Like I've never known it.

But why…? Why should that be?

Like feathers on a stream, thoughts drifted through his mind. Never before had he been a woman's first lover—and never before had a woman been his wife… nor shared his haven on Kallistris…

Were they the reasons it had seemed so…*so special*… with Rosalie?

The question hovered like a drop of rain held in the still air…and as sleep finally flowed over him it dissolved like mist. Yielding no answer.

Rosalie lay in the sun, offering her body to its warm caress. Her skin was no longer pale. The passing days had turned it to golden honey…

Five blissful, sun-kissed days!

Five even more blissful nights…

Nights of giving herself entirely to Xandros—to what they had together.

She felt her breath catch in wonder and delight.

Xandros—oh, Xandros!

She cried out his name in her head and felt her heart glow as warmly as her body.

How was it possible to be so happy?

How impossible was it not to be?

Day after day they had taken their leisure—swimming, sailing, paddleboarding, snorkelling, taking picnics up to the headland, going for easy walks amongst the wild goats through the herb-scented maquis, drinking cocktails on the beach, watching the sunset and the moonrise, feasting every evening on Maria's groaning banquets to give them strength for the long, long nights when they burned with passion and desire…finding ecstasy in each other's arms…

She felt heat beat up in her cheeks. Was it because

he was her first lover that it was so good? So special? Was that the reason?

Or was it because she had taken one look at him as she'd opened the door of that rundown rental house she'd been cleaning and known he was the most fantastic-looking male she'd ever seen in her life?

Or was it because he had swept her out of her grim, grinding poverty to bring her here, to the land of her forebears, showering upon her this amazing life of wealth and luxury, promising her that never again would she know hardship and deprivation?

She did not know why—she knew only that it was so, and that in Xandros's arms she knew a bliss that she had never imagined possible.

Why it was, she left unspoken.

Unanswered.

Xandros crunched across the pebbles, his eyes going immediately to Rosalie, sweeping over her dozing form. He felt desire quicken, as it always did, and he hunkered down beside her, indulging himself in softly brushing his hand over the soft swell of her midriff, exposed by her brief bikini.

Her eyelids fluttered open and her face broke into a smile.

He brushed her mouth with his. 'Can I tempt you to a swim before lunch?' he asked, and smiled, drawing back.

'You can tempt me to anything.' She gave an answering smile.

'Now, there's an offer!'

There was a glint in his eye as she sat up.

Today was their last day on Kallistris—they would

be heading back to Athens first thing tomorrow morning. He wasn't looking forward to it. He never liked to leave Kallistris anyway, but now his reluctance was even more marked. He'd happily spend more time here, lotus-eating with Rosalie, rather than go back in Athens, plunging head-first into all the work that making his merger with Coustakis a reality entailed.

He was conscious of the irony—after all, he had only married Rosalie to achieve the merger he wanted, and yet here he was wishing he could have more time with her here. Back in Athens he'd be putting in long days at the office and would only see her in the evenings.

Well, he would strive to make it possible to get back here as much as he could. Even a weekend would be better than nothing.

He helped her stand up now, and then stripped off to his swim shorts. Both of them waded into the waiting sea.

His thoughts went back to that first swim they'd had together. Before he had made her his own. Was it really only five days ago? They seemed to have been lovers for so much longer. It was as if they'd always been together. As if they always would be.

He frowned, wondering where that thought had come from, and dismissed it immediately as he launched into a powerful freestyle, ploughing out to sea. It was Kallistris, he thought, increasing his speed. It had that effect on him…making him forget about anywhere else. An island, indeed, of lotus-eating, where time stopped and there was neither past nor future, only an endless blissful present.

But time didn't stop in the world beyond, and back in Athens his time would be busy. His agenda non-stop.

Maybe the enchantment he was feeling with Rosalie would start to wear off there. Perhaps here, on Kallistris, where he'd never brought his amours, she seemed more special than she really was.

He left it at that, focussing on exerting his every muscle to accelerate and maintain his speed, then curving around to head back to shallower waters, where Rosalie was sedately criss-crossing the bay in a gentle breaststroke.

He dived under the water, surfacing beside her in a shower of diamond water drops, and she gave a start of surprise. He grinned, and caught her for a kiss.

'I wonder,' he said wickedly, 'what making love in the water might be like?'

She gave a gurgle of laughter. 'Leave it to the dolphins!' she quipped.

He laughed in answer, wading ashore with her.

'Okay, I'll trade it for a leisurely siesta instead,' he promised her, with a knowing glint in his eye.

Sleep would not be on the agenda…

Tomorrow morning they might be back in Athens, but for today, at least, lotus-eating and lovemaking were all he would allow.

All he wanted.

Rosalie stood gazing at her reflection. She had dressed with particular care, wanting to look her most beautiful for Xandros this evening.

Our last evening here...

A pang smote her. She was not looking forward to returning to Athens, but she knew they must. Xandros needed to get on with all the work that making his merger with her father's business entailed. That was what they had married for.

Their marriage was a means to an end—nothing more than that.

The fact that she and Xandros had become lovers was irrelevant to achieving that goal.

That is what I have to remember and never forget. The day the merger is accomplished is the day our marriage ends and we go our separate ways.

She turned away from her reflection, not wanting to see the woman there—the woman whose life had been transformed in ways she had never realised it would be when she had first landed on this beautiful enchanted island. Tomorrow they would be leaving, but she would arrive back in Athens a different person. There could be no going back to the one she had been.

She felt emotion catch at her, but let it slip away. It was best that it did. Best to simply pick up her flowered shawl and make her way out to the walled terrace. Maria, she knew, had prepared a farewell feast for them, and Xandros would be waiting for her. She must make the very most of this last evening here.

In Athens it would be…different.

She would not have his constant company…would need to be self-reliant. Already she had resolved to fill her days productively. Exploring Athens, learning Greek, and even, she had decided, picking up her online studies. Qualifications were never wasted, and when she was back in England they would come in useful even with the incredibly generous divorce settlement Xandros was promising her.

She might start her own business…make investments…

after all, she had the rest of her life ahead of her. Her life beyond Xandros…

She felt a chill strike her and pulled her shawl a little closer around her shoulders.

Yet it did not seem to warm her.

CHAPTER ELEVEN

DESPITE HER RESOLVE to be self-reliant when they were back in Athens, and not expect Xandros to dance attendance on her, Rosalie found she had to keep reminding herself that his priority was not her—it was making the merger he had married her to achieve a reality. It meant he spent long days at his office—long days in which she had to occupy herself.

She did just as she had resolved to do—assiduously exploring the city and its cornucopia of ancient treasures, attempting to learn the language as she'd told herself she would and picking up her online studies again, courtesy of the brand-new laptop Xandros had presented her with. She also, at Xandros's behest, sampled the many upmarket fashion shops in Athens in order to extend her designer wardrobe yet further—it was frivolous, but wonderful to be able to indulge herself as a budding fashionista…

After the grim, exhausting slog of her London life she knew she should only be grateful that her days now were this easy, and if her evenings alone in his apartment stretched, with Xandros often not home till late, and working weekends as well, she refused to let herself feel neglected.

She had no right to feel that way.

No right to miss him or to miss the leisurely pace they'd enjoyed on Kallistris.

On Kallistris, by day and by night, they had made slow, lingering love, with Xandros's skilled mouth and fingertips drawing from her such sensual bliss that it had been a white-out of the mind. Now there was only urgent passion, swiftly sated. When she awoke he was already up and getting ready for the office, leaving her with a brief kiss and nothing more.

She sighed, feeling guilty. She should not let herself be like this. She had so *much*! A life of ease and luxury. She had no right to feel so down. No right to want yet more.

To want Xandros to herself while she had him.

She frowned—where had *that* come from? That reminder of their time being limited. Of course it was—she'd known that from the very start! Neither of them was committed to the other except for the time they had allotted to stay together in this brief, temporary marriage.

You knew that from the start! And you knew that his focus was going to be on getting the merger done! You've no business to feel neglected or feel sorry for yourself!

But as she heard his key in the lock—early for him on this Friday evening—she felt her spirits life instantly and her mood soar. She'd seem almost nothing of him these last two weekends since returning to Athens.

Tossing his briefcase down on the sofa, Xandros swept her up into his arms. 'At last! A weekend *not* in the office!' He kissed her, and set her back, resting his hands on her shoulders. 'Time to party!' he told her.

He took a deep breath before speaking again, his words sounding heartfelt.

'I've slogged long enough—I want a break. So how about it? Let's rig ourselves up and head out! It's the birthday party of a friend of mine and I don't want to miss it—*and...*' he nodded at her and his expression was telling '...it's high time I showed you off! But first...'

His grip on her shoulders changed, becoming a caress. The expression in his face changed, too, and gold glinted in his eyes.

'But first,' he said again, 'I want to make up for all my neglect of you—'

With a catch of her breath and a quickening of her veins Rosalie realised what he intended.

His long lashes swept down over his eyes. 'Kallistris,' he said huskily, 'was far too long ago...'

His kiss was slow and sensual and melted the very bones of her. With a low laugh of triumph he surfaced, effortlessly scooping her up into his arms and carrying her through into his bedroom to lower her down upon the bed, coming down beside her.

His hand smoothed her hair from her forehead. 'Have I told you recently how very, very beautiful you are, Kyria Lakaris?'

The husk in his voice was deeper...the gold glints in his eyes more molten.

'Not recently,' she said, and sighed in warm anticipation. Gladness was filling her, arousal was beckoning, and there was another emotion, too. Relief.

He still wants me.

Had that been her fear, these last weeks? Had she thought that Xandros was turning into a workaholic not just because he had to run a multi-million-pound business doing whatever it was that he did *and* overseeing a complex and demanding merger as well? Had she not wanted to admit that she feared his attraction to her had palled?

But now, as his mouth began to glide down her throat, his fingers deftly slipping open the buttons of her shirt, of his shirt as well, his thighs moving across hers so that she felt their strength, she knew, with another sigh of pleasurable arousal, just how very keen he was to get her naked. And, beneath him, she could cast all those fears aside and glory in what came next.

A burning fusion that made her cry out again, and again as his body took her to an ecstasy that had not been hers since their last night on Kallistris.

She clung to him, shuddering in the aftermath, feeling his heart hammering as fiercely as her own, knowing his limbs were exhausted, the bedclothes in a tangled turmoil.

He pulled her tight against him. 'I must have been mad to work so hard,' he breathed. He levered himself up on his elbow. 'I'm going to take a break—for the whole weekend!' He dropped a slow kiss on her mouth. 'But tonight—tonight, Kyria Lakaris—I want you to put on the gladdest of your glad rags and make me the envy of all Athens!'

The envy of all Athens? Into her head came the jibing words her father had thrown at her when she'd defied him. It was *she* who was supposed to be the envy of all Athens…

And later, as they joined Xandros's friends in the *salon privé* at the exclusive restaurant where they were gathering, she could see that the jibe had held some truth in it. His friends were welcoming, though she found herself feeling shy, hanging on to Xandros's supporting arm, and they were happy to talk to her in English, though most of their lively conversation was conducted, understandably in Greek, but two of the most elegant women there made a beeline for her.

'We are in mourning!' they teased her. 'Xandros has been captured at last!'

'We all wanted to marry him—but he evaded us!' The nearest woman's dark eyes gleamed. 'So what is your secret?'

The other woman gave a laugh. 'The same as Ariadne's!' she exclaimed.

She seemed about to say more, but Xandros had turned away from the man whose birthday it was to drape an arm around Rosalie's shoulder.

'Come and meet the birthday boy,' he said, drawing her away. 'I want to see the envy in his eyes!'

His friend certainly showed his admiration, and Rosalie could not help but be glad she had made such an effort tonight, knowing that in such company she must do Xandros justice. Her newly purchased cocktail dress, in hues of peacock and royal blue, was, she knew, stunning in its design.

'Don't leave me alone with your wife for a second, old friend,' the birthday boy teased openly, 'or I will steal her away from you! She is ravishing!'

She smiled, knowing it for the laddish joshing that it was, but was glad of Xandros's possessive arm around her.

They took their seats for dinner at a long, formally set table laden with silverware and crystal glasses. Conversation reverted to Greek, and became very lively and good-humoured, with Xandros clearly a key player.

Part of Rosalie warmed to see him relaxed and convivial—and yet part of her ached, too, and she did not know why. And although his arm was draped around her shoulder, showing the world they were an item, she felt a distance from him.

I'm just passing through his life...and he through mine. By winter all this will be over. I'll be back in London. He'll be part of my past—nothing more than that...

She felt her throat tighten, felt memory burn. She remembered how their bodies had clung to each other in throbbing passion just a few brief hours ago…how close they'd seemed. As if nothing could part them. But time would do just that—part them in a matter of months. Just as they'd planned from the outset.

Her throat tightened again, and she felt that strange melancholy assail her as it had in his apartment, before they had married.

On Kallistris it had vanished.

Now she felt it again. More poignant.

Xandros sat back in his chair at the desk in his office and frowned. Some critical financial documentation that Stavros Coustakis should have made available to him by now had still not been sent over.

His mouth thinned. Was this the man playing yet more of his damn games? If so, his only purpose could be to flex his power just for the sake of it. After all, he'd got exactly what he'd held out for—a Lakaris son-in-law—so why the delay now? At this rate getting the merger pulled together would take irritatingly longer than Xandros had wanted it to take.

On the other hand… His expression changed. It was an ill wind that blew no one any good at all.

A delay will give me longer with Rosalie.

His dark eyes glinted appreciatively. That would definitely be a bonus—no doubt about it.

One of the things that was exacerbating his frustration with his father-in-law's dilatory co-operation over expediting the merger between them was the fact that all the demands of making it happen were keeping him in the office for far longer than he wanted.

Increasingly, he wanted to be spending time with Rosalie. Making the most of her while he had her—before they had to part company and go their own ways.

The frown was back in his eyes again. That was a pretty negative way of putting it…

And why be negative about something that's a positive?

Because of course it was *entirely* a positive that theirs was to be a temporary marriage, existing only for the purpose of making the Lakaris-Coustakis merger a reality.

It was a positive that when that happened he and Rosalie would dissolve their marriage and she would return to England, to a comfortable life of financial security. Leaving him in Greece to resume his carefree bachelor lifestyle again.

Except… His frown deepened as he sat at his desk, staring blankly at his computer screen. Except he had to admit that thought held little appeal.

Instead, his thoughts went back to the previous weekend. It had been good to take Rosalie to that birthday celebration—surprisingly good to realise that he, too, was now one of the many married couples of his acquaintance and no longer a singleton. Rosalie had seemed to enjoy herself, which was important, and though he'd heard her half-sister's name mentioned he had forestalled any deterioration of the conversation into potentially tactless discussion of Ariadne.

Anyway, it hadn't needed his arm possessively around Rosalie to show all his friends the convincing proof that Ariadne was history and why. They'd all been able to see how blown away he was by Rosalie—and not just because of her stunning beauty, or the way he only had to look at her to want to sweep her off to bed.

I enjoy her company.

He'd known that from the start, he realised—even before he'd claimed her for his own. She was easy to be with…enjoyable to be with. *Good* to be with. Good to spend time with.

They'd done a lot of that over the weekend. Spending time together. On the Saturday, the day after the birthday bash, they'd piled into his car and taken off across the Corinth Canal into the Peloponnese, down past the ancient sites of Mycenae and Epidaurus.

Rosalie's eyes had widened as he'd told her the tales and the history he'd grown up with, which she hungered for to make up for her missing birthright.

They'd spent the night in Naphlion, Greece's first capital after regaining its modern independence, and Rosalie had been enchanted by the graceful old houses and peaceful squares there. It had been good—very good—to wander with her, hand in hand, exploring the narrow streets and byways, taking their time, taking their ease, enjoying it all…

He wished he could look forward to taking her sightseeing the whole of the coming weekend. But that wasn't going to be possible. Not because he would be tied to his desk, working on the merger, but because his mother had invited them to lunch on Saturday.

He knew he couldn't get out of it. His mother needed to meet Rosalie—if for no other reason than to forestall any potential gossip that she was ostracising her new daughter-in-law. To stop any rumours that she wasn't meeting Rosalie because she expected the marriage to be of short duration. *That* must definitely not get back to Stavros!

Xandros gave a resigned sigh. He hoped his mother would go easy on Rosalie…not make her preference for Ariadne too obvious. Had she heard from Rosalie's sister yet? he wondered, and then put the question aside. Ariadne would surface when she was good and ready, and he wished her well. But between her and Rosalie there was no comparison. None at all.

How could he ever have seriously contemplated marrying Ariadne? It seemed absurd now. Now that he had Rosalie…

While he had her…

Without his being aware of it, the frown had come back to his eyes…even before his secretary had put her head around his door to tell him that the Coustakis accounts he'd been so impatient for had still not arrived.

Stavros's delays were not all that displeased him…

Rosalie's eyes widened as Xandros nosed his car down the long drive and his mother's home came into sight. This was not a house—it was a mansion! More like the Greek equivalent of an English stately home. The large three-storey edifice was set in equally spacious grounds, deep in the countryside to the north of Athens. Tall cypresses flanked it on either side, and a large stone ornamental pond with a trickling fountain fronted it as they crunched along the gravel drive.

'It was built in the nineteenth century,' Xandros was telling her, 'by my great-great-grandfather, after the creation of the modern Greek state. I grew up here.' He paused. 'I was very fortunate to be able to do so,' he went on.

His voice had changed, Rosalie could hear, and she looked at him questioningly.

He caught her look and gave her a faint smile as he drew up in front of the grand front entrance. 'It very nearly had to be sold,' he said. He switched off the car's engine, looking at her. 'My grandfather lived very extravagantly, and it was my father who had to battle to save the family fortune. It was touch-and-go all my boyhood. He succeeded, but…' His expression tightened. 'It shortened his life…all the stress he was under for so long. That is why, you see, I'm so very keen on making this merger with your father happen. I never want the kind of financial worry I grew up with to affect my family again.'

His expression changed again, and his voice became apologetic.

'I know that probably sounds…well, *insulting* to you, given what you and your poor mother had to put up with all your lives—'

She shook her head. 'No…' she answered slowly. 'I think it explains why you've been so kind to me—why you don't want me to be poor again.'

It did, she realised. In his own way he felt a degree of similarity between them, vastly different though their backgrounds had been. And, she thought—and it was a strange thought, given that vast difference—it also made her understand how similarly driven he was, how dogged his determination to achieve the merger he sought by whatever means necessary.

Just as I was determined to lift myself out of poverty by whatever means necessary. Whether that was by working my guts out as a cleaner to fund my studies or by marrying...

Her expression flickered. Was that why she'd married Xandros? The only reason? Truly the only reason…?

The question hovered and she was unwilling to seek an answer. Was grateful that he was now giving a rueful smile to her response.

'Well, it is kind of you to say so,' he replied. 'And I hope you can be as forbearing with my mother.' His mouth tightened. 'I need to tell you that Ariadne's mother was a good friend of hers, and for that reason my mother shared your father's enthusiasm for my marrying your half-sister. She accepts that Ariadne did not share that enthusiasm, but—'

He broke off. The grand front door was opening, and a butler—or so Rosalie surmised—was emerging. Xandros got out, greeted the stately personage and came round to open Rosalie's door.

She got out, nerves pinching. This was an ancestral home, by any standards, but it was strange to think of what Xandros had just disclosed—that the wealth he so obviously enjoyed had not always been guaranteed. Strange, too—and more disturbing—to think that Xandros's mother had wanted Xandros to marry Ariadne, just as her father had, even though Xandros and Ariadne had clearly had no intention of going along with either parent's wishes.

Butterflies fluttered in her stomach. It wasn't going to make it any easier to cope with the forthcoming meeting. But at least she had the comfort of knowing that Xandros's mother knew just how artificial their marriage was.

She was glad she had dressed with extreme care, in a modestly styled dress, and had applied equally modest make-up. And she was glad when Xandros gave her hand a reassuring squeeze as the stately butler showed them in to a drawing room whose elegance matched the grand house.

The woman greeting them was equally elegant.

'My dear…' Kyria Lakaris said faintly, her smile even fainter, and then she smiled far more warmly at her son when Xandros kissed her cheek.

He made most of the conversation during the visit, sticking to anodyne subjects such as their recent venture into the Peloponnese, and Rosalie was thankful. Though he kept mostly to English, his mother very often replied in Greek.

Is she trying to shut me out, or am I being oversensitive?

She gave a mental shrug, because in the end what did it matter whether Xandros's mother disapproved of her? Disapproved of her son marrying her? She would be gone out of his life soon enough.

Several times during the laborious luncheon they sat through, in a dining room as elegant as the drawing room, she heard her half-sister's name from her mother-in-law, and she could tell by his tone of his voice, even in Greek, that Xandros's replies were terse. He always pointedly reverted to English, making some remark about his boyhood.

It was the only subject that drew a response from his mother—the first sign of animation Rosalie had seen in her yet.

'This is a wonderful place for a child to grow up—so much space to run around in! And for the next generation, too. I so look forward to seeing my grandchildren here,' his mother commented, looking at Rosalie. 'Of course, had Xandros married Ariadne—'

Xandros's voice cut across her, saying something repressive in Greek. His mother's mouth tightened, but she did not continue.

Rosalie had got the message, though. Well, Xandros's mother would have to wait for her grandchildren—wait until her son was free of his current marriage.

Wait until he marries again. To a real wife this time, so they can make a life together...have children... Xandros's children...

She snapped her mind away. Xandros's future children were nothing to do with her. There was no point, was there, in her sudden vision of a pair of toddlers running about in the sun-drenched gardens beyond the dining room windows…?

She would be gone from his life by then…

Long gone.

Her gaze flickered out to the gardens again, and she felt an inexplicable tightening of her throat assail her.

She longed for the lunch to be over, and finally it was. It was with a real sense of relief that she drove off with Xandros.

'Thank you,' he said, 'for coping with my mother.'

His expression was speaking volumes, and Rosalie was appreciative.

'She's bound to be concerned by the nature of our

marriage,' she answered generously. 'She's protective of you. It's understandable.'

He cast her a glance. 'Thank you for that,' he said. 'You see,' he went on, and Rosalie could hear the constraint in his voice, 'she is very fond of Ariadne, and she's worried by her continued silence. I've told her your half-sister will surface when she is good and ready to do so.'

'I hope she does.' Rosalie's voice was warm. 'I long to meet her! It would be lovely to do so before I leave Greece!'

She turned away, looking out over the countryside, at the fields and the ubiquitous olive groves baking in the afternoon sun. It was high summer now. Time was passing. The inevitable date of her departure was that much closer.

'How is the merger coming along?' she heard herself ask, looking back at Xandros.

That, after all, was setting the timetable for the duration of their marriage. Like a ticking clock, counting down the hours…the days…the weeks and months… until there was no further need for them to be married.

No reason for them to be together…

He changed gear, revving the engine and picking up speed. His expression tightened.

'Not as fast as I'd hoped. Your father isn't exactly rushing to complete it. He keeps me waiting for essential information and so on.'

She saw him give a shrug, and was aware, though she knew she shouldn't be, that there was an upside to any delay. An upside for *her*, at least…

It put back, just a little, the ticking clock of their marriage…

Xandros was still speaking, and she shook the forbidden thought from her head.

'Doubtless it's all just one of his power plays—he likes to stay in control of things…and people.' A sympathetic glance came her way. 'As you know to your cost.' He changed gear again, speeding up even more. 'But we'll get there.' His expression lightened. 'Anyway, let's not waste what's left of the weekend dwelling on it! We'll take the scenic route back to the city—I can show you some more sights.'

They did just that, taking in the ancient sites of Eleusis and Megaris, and Rosalie enjoyed every minute. But then, she thought wryly, she would enjoy going round an industrial estate if it was with Xandros…

I just like being with him—anywhere, any time…

But nowhere he had yet taken her, either now or on the previous weekend, however glorious and spectacular in terms of sightseeing, could compare with Kallistris.

Will we ever get back there?

Yearning filled her. A yearning that maybe he picked up on telepathically, because when they stopped for coffee, midafternoon, he glanced at her and said, 'Let's try and get away to Kallistris before much longer, shall we? Get in a weekend there? Would that be good?'

Rosalie's face lit, and she answered enthusiastically.

In the end it was another fortnight before they could get back to Kallistris, but when they did it was every bit as good as she remembered. The island was as beautiful as ever, the little beach was as beautiful as ever, the simple whitewashed villa as beautiful as ever, the sea was as crystal clear as ever, the sun as hot as ever.

The two days passed in a flash—not nearly long enough—though they did nothing except swim and sail and sun themselves and be fed gargantuan meals by Maria.

I want more—so much more! And not just of Kallistris. Of Xandros. For much, much longer...

She knew she shouldn't feel that way, but she could not stop herself.

I don't want this time with Xandros to end! I want it to go on and on!

But how could she want that when it had been no part of their agreement? When the clock was ticking inexorably towards the time when there would be no purpose to their marriage any more.

Yet she could not deny the truth of it to herself. And it was a truth that continued to pluck at her on their return to Athens, when she resumed the life she'd got used to there.

Days passed into weeks, with Xandros again putting in long hours at work, interspersing them with short, intense periods of being with her.

Sometimes they managed to get to Kallistris at the weekend; more often, though, it was just driving out to explore yet more of Greece with him—up to Delphi, famed for its oracle, and out to the long island of Euboea, across the dramatic Gulf of Corinth bridge to visit the site of the ancient Olympic games.

Sometimes they stayed in Athens, taking it easy in the apartment, with long lie-ins and vegging in front of the TV, tuned to an English-language channel or watching online movies. Or dining out *à deux* in beautiful restaurants. Or socialising at a dinner dance, or another grand and glittering affair.

And, although it was a thrill to dress up so finely, she knew that it was because she was with Xandros that she enjoyed them so much.

Her days were still solitary, but she didn't mind. Some of Xandros's female friends had asked her to lunch, but she'd never gone. She didn't want to be stand-offish, but she was worried that without Xandros to shelter her she might let it slip that she would not be making her life with him.

It was safer to keep her own company. Just as she was today, settling down at her favourite pavement café for lunch.

She was making dogged progress with her self-taught Greek-language lessons, aided by books and podcasts, and she tried it out assiduously as she went around Athens, or even on Xandros himself. Now she unfolded the easy-read tabloid newspaper she'd just bought, a dictionary to hand, to see what she could manage of its articles.

A shadow fell across her as she pursed her lips, making out an unfamiliar word in the headline. She assumed it was the waiter, coming to take her order, and looked up with a smile.

It froze on her face.

It was her father.

CHAPTER TWELVE

SHOCK AND DISMAY jolted through her. She had not set eyes on him since she had stormed out that hideous morning after he'd ripped all her stupid dreams to pieces.

Without asking, he sat himself down.

'So,' he said, his English strong and accented, 'my dutiful daughter.'

His voice was as unmelodious as she recalled, and there was a mocking look in his pouched eyes. Rosalie could say nothing, could only feel the mix of shock and dismay possessing her.

'What? No kiss for your devoted father? The father who got you such a rich and handsome husband?' The mockery came again, along with a jibing twist to his voice. 'I *knew* you'd see sense and marry him—I didn't keep you in poverty so you wouldn't know what side your bread's buttered on! You like the luxury life, just like everyone does,' he sneered.

'What do you want?' Her voice was terse and tight. She could feel her heart starting to hammer in her chest.

His heavy eyebrows rose. 'Want? What do you *think* I want?'

His grey-green eyes, so like hers though he himself was nothing like her—*nothing*—bored into her.

'I want what I have told you I want. I've got half of it—my fancy Lakaris son-in-law. Now I want the rest.'

He leaned forward, his piercing gaze working over her, resting on her abdomen assessingly before coming back to her still-frozen expressionless face.

'I want my Lakaris grandson,' he said. His eyes narrowed. 'Are you breeding yet? You've had long enough for that fine husband of yours to play the ram!'

Rosalie gasped—not at his crudeness, but at what he'd said.

He gave a coarse laugh. 'Did you think I'd be content with him just putting a ring on your finger? He'll have to put a baby in your belly, too! So,' he repeated, 'are you breeding yet? It's a simple question and a crucial one.' There was a look of relish in his face now, as if he were enjoying what he was telling her. 'Crucial for that handsome husband of yours, that is!'

She swallowed. Her heart was still hammering in her chest. 'What…what do you mean?'

'Crucial,' her father answered, 'if he wants to complete this precious merger he's after.' He cocked his head, surveying her with his heavy-lidded gaze as if he were a snake and she a cornered mouse. 'No baby, no completion,' he spelt out.

He got to his feet, looking down at her as icy water pooled in her stomach.

'Tell him that!' His mouth gave that cruel twist again. 'And as for you—how long do you think you'll last as his dressed-up doll of a wife if you can't bring him the one thing he married you for? Getting his hands on my business! And don't think to come running to *me* if he discards you. I won't lift a finger. You can get back to your London slum and starve again! So,' he finished, turning away, 'get yourself pregnant, my girl—if you want to stay in the lap of this luxury you've grabbed with both hands.'

He walked away. Climbed into the tinted-windowed car idling at the kerb, which drove off.

Leaving Rosalie sick with dismay.

Across the ancient city the floodlit Parthenon blazed on the Acropolis. But Rosalie, standing on the balcony of Xandros's apartment, her hands clutching the railing, was blind to it. Blind and deaf to everything except the thought pounding in her head like a merciless drum.

You have to tell him—you have to tell him.

She had to tell Xandros what her father had said. Threatened. Because it had been a threat—a stark and ruthless threat. No baby—no merger.

She felt her stomach clench.

We thought we were outmanoeuvring him...turning the tables on him. Now he's turned them back on us!

The feeling of sick dismay that had filled her at her father's words was there again, and she could not rid herself of it. How could she not dread having to tell Xandros…? Tell him that their marriage had been pointless all along. That the merger he wanted so badly was going to be impossible to achieve.

I have to tell him! But I can't—not yet! Not tonight!

She wanted—craved—a little longer with him before she had to shatter his hopes. Just a little longer…

With a smothered cry, she wrenched herself away, hurrying indoors. Xandros would be home soon, and she had to change for the dinner dance they were going to tonight. She had another new evening gown to show off to him. She must look as beautiful as she always strove to look for him—had to see his eyes light and glint with admiration and desire…

Just give me tonight with him! I'll tell him tomorrow—in the morning...

As though it might be easier then… When it was going to be the hardest thing in the world.

Xandros was leading her out onto the dance floor, taking her into his arms. Rosalie's eyes clung to him. He was looking as superb as he always looked in black tie, and she knew by the expression in his eyes as he gazed down at her that she was spectacular, in a sumptuous off-the-shoulder gown in champagne satin, with diamond drops at her ears, her hair upswept into an elaborate style, her make-up full and dramatic.

All around were couples equally resplendent, and chandeliers glittered above them as Xandros swept her away into the dance. Rosalie clung to him as he whirled her around—a former Cinderella at yet another lavish ball, dancing the night away with the most handsome man in the room. Her very own prince… Living the high life. Living the dream…

But what was the dream? What would it be worth to me, all this lavish luxury, if I wasn't here with Xandros?

She heard the question in her head as her gaze drank him in. Her fingers tightened on his sleeve as she leaned into his tall, hard body with unconscious closeness. She knew, without any shadow of a doubt, and with a catch in her heart that tightened the vice that had been squeezing around her ever since that ugly confrontation with her father, that without Xandros none of this glitter and glitz and luxury and wealth would be anything at all!

It's Xandros I want—and I would want him even if we were living as simply as Maria and Panos do. It would be paradise enough because I would be with Xandros.

But what use was it, that searing self-knowledge?

It was true for *her*, not him!

She might want Xandros only for himself—not for the freedom from poverty he promised her, not for the taste of luxury she was enjoying in this time she had with him—but he saw it very differently.

The vice tightened around her heart again.

He wants me only as a gateway to his merger with my father's business.

And if that gateway slammed shut Xandros would end their marriage. There would be no reason to continue it.

Unless…

As she gazed up at Xandros in the whirl of the dance she felt a rush of emotion so intense she could not bear it. Felt a temptation she could hardly dare give thought to. Yet it burned in her head…

What if I don't tell Xandros? If I never tell him my father's impossible demand?

The thought swirled through her as the music whirled them about—a thought that stung her conscience like a wasp.

I could do what my father wants—it would be so easy...

Since their honeymoon she had taken responsibility for contraception by going on the Pill. All she had to do was stop taking it…

Yearning filled her. Oh, to have Xandros's baby!

To know that she could stay with him for ever! Make a family with him!

Longing possessed her, fierce and urgent—urging. *You could do it—it would be easy...so easy...*

And totally unforgivable.

Xandros grinned at the antics of Panos and Maria's young grandchildren, who were visiting with their mother. It had been an impulsive notion for him and Rosalie to head to Kallistris this morning, after last night's dinner-dance, but well worth it—as it always was.

His eyes went to her now, warming as they did so. She, like him, was smiling at the two toddlers, the older one petting Panos's dogs, the younger stalking a chicken. Xandros made an admiring comment to the doting grandparents, and offered his congratulations on being informed that their daughter was expecting once again.

His glance went to the children's mother, now rescuing the chicken from her daughter's attentions. Her pregnancy didn't show yet, but then Maria's daughter had inherited her mother's fuller figure. His glance travelled on to Rosalie. *She* was so slender that pregnancy would show immediately…

He caught his thoughts. The very idea of Rosalie pregnant—

'Shall we head down to the beach for a swim?' he asked her, to push away a thought that had no business being there.

They took their leave and padded down the trackway to the villa companionably, hand in hand. He'd half expected Rosalie to make some comment about the cuteness of Maria and Panos's grandchildren, but she was silent. He glanced at her sideways. Her face was slightly drawn…as if she were lost in thought. Perhaps she wasn't making any remark about the toddlers for the same reason as he. Because pregnancy, babies, children were absolutely nothing to do with themselves…

He felt the thought move in his head, found himself squeezing her hand more tightly, as if not to let her go.

But I'm going to have to let her go sometime, aren't I? Once the merger is done.

A frown formed on his brow and his glance went to her again. From Panos and Maria's smallholding he could still hear the gleeful laughter of the toddlers. The sound tugged at him. Thoughts came unbidden…

What if they were ours? Mine and Rosalie's? What if we were making our lives together, making a family together for ever?

The questions hung in his head. Motionless. Unanswerable.

His gaze slipped across to the blue horizon over the sea. Gulls were swooping and hovering, borne aloft on the air currents. Suddenly, one folded its wings and dived, plunging down into the water as if it had seen something it wanted. Something invisible to Xandros but there beneath the surface.

All he had to do was do as the gull had done and find what he was seeking. The answer to his wondering question…

Rosalie was staring into thin air, her hands clenched in her lap. Tonight—she must tell Xandros what her father had said tonight! She *must*. Before the unforgivable temptation that had swept over her as she'd danced in his arms and that had kept on coming back over and over again all through the weekend became too overwhelming to resist. A temptation made even more powerful by seeing Maria and Panos's grandchildren…so adorable, so enviable!

He has to know! He has to!

But, oh, she did not want to tell him! She wanted to go on as they were for just a little longer…a *little* longer…

One more weekend on Kallistris…and another…and another…

How can I bear to ruin what we have? To end it so much sooner than it has to end by telling him how impossible it is to complete the merger he's set his heart on? The merger we married to achieve. The sole purpose of our marriage…

Unless…

The word hung in her head again, testing her to the utmost—tempting her to the utmost. She felt anguish fill her, her hands clenching again in her lap.

A sudden sound distracted her hopeless thoughts. The phone was ringing. The apartment's landline, not her mobile.

She frowned. If it was Xandros, he'd use her mobile number. He'd flown up to Thessaloniki for the day, to meet with some of her father's senior managers based there to discuss the staffing implications of the merger when it happened.

But it can't happen, can it? Not now.

Everything Xandros was doing was a waste of his time.

I have to tell him—I just have to…

The landline went on ringing, despite her nerve-racking thoughts, and she got up reluctantly to answer it.

'Parakelo?' she said, hoping she would not get a volley of Greek beyond her capabilities from someone wanting to speak to Xandros.

But the call was for her.

'Rosalie?'

The voice was female—and recognisable. It was Xandros's mother.

Surprise filled Rosalie—and a sudden apprehension. 'Kyria Lakaris?'

'Yes. My dear…'

There was a slight pause, as if Xandros's mother was deciding what to say, and that bite of apprehension came again. Never before had Xandros's mother phoned her, so why…?

Something's happened to Xandros!

Apprehension sharpened to fear…

'I am in the lobby. May I come up?' asked Xandros's mother.

Fear subsided into wariness.

'Yes—yes, of course,' she replied.

The line went dead, and Rosalie opened the apartment door just as the lift doors opened to reveal Xandros's mother.

Politely she stood aside, to let her enter her son's apartment. Her mother-in-law—the very last person Rosalie had expected to see—seemed agitated. Apprehension bit at Rosalie again.

'My dear, I need to speak to you,' Xandros's mother said.

She sat herself down on one of the sofas, and Rosalie lowered herself tensely to the other.

'Has something happened?' she heard herself ask, not able to keep the alarm out of her voice. 'To Xandros?'

The older Kyria Lakaris shook her head. 'No,' she said quickly.

Too quickly, Rosalie thought. Something *had* happened—something that was not good.

Yet what her mother-in-law said next reversed that thought instantly.

'My dear, Ariadne has returned!'

Rosalie's face lit. 'Oh, I'm so glad! I know you were very worried about her.'

Xandros's mother nodded. But her demeanour was still agitated, and she went on speaking rapidly. 'Yes... yes, I *was* worried indeed. But she has been, as Xandros thought, with her relatives in Scotland. Now, though, she is back in Greece—she arrived at the weekend. She came to me because of her...estrangement...from her father—' She broke off.

'He has behaved very badly towards her,' Rosalie said, wanting to make it clear where her sympathies lay. Her face lit again. 'I do hope so very much, though, that Ariadne will want to meet me. I've been longing to meet *her*—'

Xandros's mother cut across her, her expression constrained. 'That would not be...advisable,' she said, as if searching for the right word. 'You see...' The expression of constraint deepened and she pressed her lips tightly for a moment. 'Ariadne is pregnant.'

Rosalie stared. She could not think of anything to say except, 'That's wonderful!'

Xandros's mother was looking at her strangely. 'That's a very generous thing to say...' she said slowly.

Rosalie stared. 'I don't understand. Why is it generous?'

'You are generous,' said Xandros's mother, 'to be so understanding of the predicament your predecessor finds herself in.'

'My…my predecessor?' Rosalie's voice was hollow.

'Of course,' Kyria Lakaris was saying. 'Ariadne was engaged to my son until the moment she disappeared.'

The world seemed to tip on its axis, dislodging everything in it. Everything except one single word.

'Engaged?'

It fell like a ton weight from Rosalie's lips. She stared at Xandros's mother. Shock was knifing through her.

Kyria Lakaris looked at her frowningly. 'Did you not know?' she was saying. 'The wedding was all set—it was a great blow to him when she ran away…broke off the engagement.'

'They were *engaged*?' Rosalie could only echo the word again. Inside, shock was detonating, reaching all her limbs so that she was weak from it. 'He…he told me that Ariadne refused point-blank to entertain our father's obsession—'

But Kyria Lakaris was shaking her head in negation. 'My dear—no. Just the opposite. She was perfectly willing to marry Xandros.'

'But Xandros…Xandros said he would never be manipulated by my father! He came to London to tell me so!' Rosalie was gasping, snatching at all the things Xandros had said to her.

His mother was shaking her head again, contradicting her with the gesture. 'That was after Ariadne panicked. Pre-wedding nerves—I'm sure it was only that! Had Xandros not gone chasing to London, I am quite,

quite sure Ariadne would have seen sense and come home.' Regret was audible in the older woman's voice as she went on, 'They were ideally suited to each other, your half-sister and my son.'

Then, in front of Rosalie's stricken eyes, Kyria Lakaris's face brightened.

'And now they can be once more!' she exclaimed.

Rosalie stared. 'I don't understand...' she said slowly, each word dragged from her. 'You...you've just told me that Ariadne is...is pregnant. So how can she and Xandros ever...ever get back together?'

His mother's expression had changed. It was filled now with a new emotion. It was pity. Chilling Rosalie to the core.

And a moment later she knew why.

'You have been married to Xandros for less than three months,' Xandros's mother said. 'And Ariadne...' She paused for a moment, her eyes holding Rosalie's with a painful expression. 'Ariadne has had her first trimester confirmed. So you see...' she took a breath '...there can be no question about it—your half-sister carries my son's child.'

CHAPTER THIRTEEN

XANDROS THREW HIMSELF down on the hotel bed in Thessaloniki. He'd just had a brilliant idea. He would phone Rosalie, explain that he needed to spend another day here at the Coustakis offices—the managers there had been only just been briefed by Stavros, in another damn delaying tactic of the man!—and suggest she fly up here tomorrow to join him. Then, his meetings over, he would hire a car and take off with her to explore the countryside of north-eastern Greece.

Hell, if Stavros was in no rush to get the merger done, why should he be?

It would give him yet more time with Rosalie—taking the next few days to show her the resorts of the trident-shaped Halkidiki, with the extraordinary monastery atop Mount Athos. Even get to Macedonia and show her the fabulous tomb of Alexander the Great's father, with its treasure trove of gold filigree ornaments.

He smiled at the prospect. Two days—maybe more if they felt like it!—of the non-stop company of the one person he wanted to be with!

Rosalie.

Rosalie, Rosalie, Rosalie—her very name was a delight! Just as *she* was a delight! All of her—all the time. In every way…

He felt emotion well up in him. The same emotion he'd felt last Sunday afternoon, when he'd imagined what it would be like if it were Rosalie who was pregnant, not Maria's daughter. Say, just by chance…

Or even not by chance…

What then…?

The implications hovered in his head, spreading out through his consciousness, filling his mind.

We'd stay together, obviously—keep our marriage going...

Okay, that wasn't what they'd originally planned—not what he'd intended or wanted—but that had been then…not now.

His expression changed. Now things were different. His time with Rosalie had changed him.

Had it changed his plans, his intentions as well?

Changed what he felt about marriage?

About Rosalie?

Into his head came what he'd said to her when she'd praised the lifestyle Panos and Maria enjoyed.

'Sometimes when you have too much of something you enjoy it palls...'

He frowned. Was that true of his time with Rosalie? Would the time come when he had had too much of her, so that being with her palled?

It seemed an absurd question!

Do I really want our marriage to end when the merger is done?

His eyes flickered.

A baby would keep us together...

A child with Rosalie…

He turned over the thought in his mind.

Enticing. Appealing…

Perhaps, he mused, gazing up at the ceiling, lost in this strangely beguiling thought, when she joined him here he would draw her out on the subject… On the subject of not rushing to end their marriage. At all.

I need to know! To know what she feels—what she wants.

Surely he was not hoping in vain?

Memory was full within him—of the passion and desire in their lovemaking, the way her beautiful body clung to his, the heights they reached together every time! And it was more than when they were in bed—in and out of bed it was the same. Her smiles, her laughter, her kisses and her conversation… Surely it all pointed to the same thoughts, the same feelings, that were filling him more and more with every passing day…every passionate night…?

I want her with me all the time! Every day and every night! And I want her to want the same!

It was as though a light had gone on in his head, showing him things he'd never seen before…things that were now illuminated in a brilliant golden light. He reached for his phone to call her, to hear her voice, ask her to fly up here.

Before he could pick it up, it started to ring. He grinned. Was Rosalie telepathic as well as all her other manifold charms?

But as he answered, and heard the voice of his caller, his smile was wiped from his face.

'Ariadne?'

He jackknifed upright.

Her voice came clear over the ether. Sounding fraught.

'Xandros! I've got something to tell you. And it can't wait. It just can't!'

Everything in him froze.

Rosalie squirted cleaning fluid into the bathtub, and started to scrub the inside, her movements as automatic as they were familiar. Anguish filled her—and not just because she was right back where she'd started: in London, broke and cleaning for a living. Just the way Xandros had first found her.

That was her anguish—that single word, his name.

Xandros—the man she loved.

That was the truth of it—bitter now as gall. With every golden day she had spent with Xandros—every passion-fuelled night—the truth had been coming to her. Deny it as she had—suppress it as she'd had to.

We married to make the merger happen. But for me it became more—so much more.

How could it not? Pain shot through her. How could she *not* have done what she had, day after day, night after night? How could she *not* have fallen in love with Xandros? Weaving dreams that their brief marriage might last instead of ending?

That we might make our whole lives together—have children, a future... It was a dream I longed for so much that the temptation to make it happen was almost impossible to resist!

Cold shivered through her. Her punishment for so very nearly yielding to the unforgivable temptation to let herself get pregnant...have Xandros's baby, bind him to her for ever...was unbearable.

It would be her half-sister who would have his baby now.

The half-sister who, far from refusing outright even to countenance marrying Xandros, had in fact been willing—as willing as Xandros had been to take Ariadne to his bed as his fiancée…

A corrosive sickness filled Rosalie, as if she had swallowed the bleach she was cleaning the bathtub with, and into her aching head came his mother's oft-repeated words: *'They were ideally suited to each other...'* And now they could be again. *I must hope with all my heart that whatever made Ariadne run away, reject Xandros, she can now find happiness with him! The happiness they must have felt when they agreed to marry. Why should they not be happy? They will have everything—each other, their baby, even the merger...*

Because her father would have got what he wanted: a Lakaris son-in-law and a Lakaris grandchild—with the daughter he'd originally wanted to have them.

Pain smote her yet again.

Ariadne would have everything.

And I will have nothing.

Only her memories. Her broken dreams. Her broken heart.

Useless tears smarted in her eyes and she rubbed them away with the back of her rubber-gloved hand. Went on with her cleaning.

After all, there was nothing else for her to do now…

The phone was ringing on his desk, and Xandros snatched it up on its first ring. It was his lawyer. The last person to have seen Rosalie the day she'd disappeared—saying she was filing for divorce.

The word still bit like a shark and he could not shake it off. Its jaws were clamped around him, drawing blood…

'Any news?' he demanded.

His adrenaline levels were sky-high—had been ever since Ariadne had phoned him in Thessaloniki, two weeks ago now. Ever since he'd received Rosalie's text shortly thereafter.

Xandros, your mother has told me about Ariadne, so I'm going back to London today.

Emotion convulsed in him. It was like some bitterly ironic replay. Ariadne had texted to say she was fleeing from him. Now Rosalie had done the same.

Except that it isn't the same at all! Not by a million miles—not by all the distance between the galaxies!

When Ariadne had fled all he had felt was relief.

With Rosalie it was…

Desperation.

As brutal as that.

Clutching him, crushing him.

He took a ragged breath now, the phone clamped to his ear.

'We have received a contact address,' came the reply.

'Finally!' breathed Xandros, relief flooding through him.

Five minutes later he'd booked a flight to London—into whose anonymous millions Rosalie had simply… disappeared.

Despite his urgent efforts there had been no trace of her. Not at the dive she'd used to live in, nor at the cleaning agency she'd worked for. She'd just…vanished.

But now—at last—she'd shown up!

He punched in the number for Ariadne and she answered immediately, anxious to hear from him.

'She's got in touch! Told the lawyer how to reach her,' he announced. 'So I'm flying straight off to London now.'

But his buoyant relief did not last beyond his hot-footed arrival at the hotel she'd given as her contact address. Where she awaited the paperwork that she expected him to send her so as to expedite the divorce she was initiating.

He stared disbelievingly at the reception desk clerk.

'But she *must* be staying here—she's given this hotel as her address!'

It wasn't the same hotel he'd taken her to that first night he'd found her, because he'd already checked there. And now she didn't seem to be at this one either.

Frustration knifed in him—and anxiety, too. The credit card he'd given her when they'd married hadn't been used—so how was she paying for whatever accommodation she was in? The last thing he wanted was her resorting to her own meagre finances… Especially after what she'd told his lawyer—

He snapped his mind away—back to what the hotel clerk was repeating to him.

'I am so sorry, Mr Lakaris, but there is absolutely no record of Mrs Lakaris as a current or recent guest.'

Nor had she booked in under her maiden name—or the Coustakis name.

Grim-faced, he checked into the hotel himself, going up to his room with a heavy frown. He shrugged off his jacket, threw himself down on the bed.

Where is she?

The question burned in him, finding no answer.

Where to look next?

She could be anywhere! Anywhere at all!

A discreet knock sounded on the door. Irritated at the disturbance, he got up, strode to the door and yanked it open. It was Housekeeping. The turn-down service.

Except the chambermaid who stood there gasped in shocked dismay.

It was Rosalie.

The blood was draining from Rosalie's face, and faintness drummed in her ears.

She could not move…was frozen to the spot with shock.

With dismay.

With something that was the very opposite of dismay…

And then Xandros was seizing her, dragging her into the room, holding her by her shoulders.

'Rosalie? What the *hell*?'

She heard words breaking from him.

'So that's why there's no trace of you here as a *guest*!' He was staring at her, shock in his face. 'How can you possibly be working *here*?' he demanded.

'They…they provide accommodation for housekeeping staff,' she said falteringly. 'I gave up my old bedsit when—'

He cut across her, an expletive breaking from him and then a volley of vehement Greek.

'We have to talk,' he said grimly.

He propelled her to the room's armchair, pressing her down into it. Her legs were like jelly and she sank down heavily. It was as if a storm was breaking out in her head.

Xandros towered over her.

'Why the *hell* did you leave Athens like that? Without talking to me first?' he demanded.

His eyes were like black pits, his face stark.

'To say *what*, Xandros?' she cried in reply.

Her heart was hammering, each beat a blow hard enough to crush her to the ground.

It was unbearable to see him.

I thought I would never set eyes on him again.

Pain clutched at her at the thought—and at the reality of seeing him. Because there was no reason for him to have sought her! No point—no purpose.

No purpose in anything now except what she had to do now—what she was telling him, the words tearing from her.

'It was obvious what I had to do. I had to set you free!' She swallowed, and there was a razor blade in her throat, drawing blood. 'Free to marry Ariadne.' Her voice changed. 'As you always wanted to.'

He was staring at her, his brows snapping together in an uncomprehending black frown. He lowered himself to the bed, leaning forward. In the low light his features seemed gaunt and strained, and tension racked his jacketless shoulders.

Helplessly, she let her eyes rest on the way his powerful chest moulded the fine material of his shirt… Then she dragged her pointless gaze away. He was gone from her—as distant as the stars in the sky. All she had to do now was tell him that she knew that, accepted it…

'Your mother told me, Xandros!' she said, her voice

twisting painfully. 'Told me what I had absolutely no idea of! That you and Ariadne were once *engaged*!'

'My mother—' His voice was bitter.

'Xandros! Don't blame her! I'm grateful to her—incredibly grateful! She was as kind as she could possibly have been about it! She was upset—I could see she was. Upset for me as well as upset because obviously the whole situation is a mess! An unholy, hideous mess!' A cry broke from her. 'If *only* you hadn't given up on Ariadne! She'd have come back to you—as she has now—and then…then everything would have been all right.'

She took a gulping breath, leaning forward, willing him to hear her out. To know she was doing all she could to clear up that unholy, hideous mess. The mess that had Xandros married to one woman while another carried his child. The woman he had wanted to marry all along…

'But it still will be all right,' she said urgently now. 'I'll do everything I can to get our divorce through as fast as it can be done, I promise! And as for the pre-nup—of course I won't be taking a penny from you!' She swallowed. 'Not now you don't need me to get your merger with my father.'

Her face worked. She knew she had to say this, too. That it would make it easier for him in the long run.

'There's something I haven't told you. I was… I was going to steel myself to do it, but I didn't want to spoil that last weekend on Kallistris. My father cornered me in a café the day before and he told me…' Her voice faltered, but she forced herself on. 'He told me that he would not progress the merger until—' Her voice cracked with the pain of it all and the bitter, bitter irony. 'Until he knew that I was pregnant.'

She clenched her hands together, twisting her fingers tightly in her misery. She made herself meet those blank dark eyes that were resting on her with a weight she could not bear. Crushing the air in her lungs, making it impossible to speak. Yet speak she must. Her eyes were huge, imploring him to understand.

'So, you see, Xandros…' She faltered once more, and then went on—because what else was there to do now but play it out to the bitter end? Even though it was tearing her into ragged shreds. 'When your mother told me about Ariadne… Well, it's all worked out for the best, hasn't it?' Her voice flattened, and she forced herself on. 'Everything has come together just the way you originally wanted! And for my father, too—so he won't delay things any more. You'll get your merger and you'll get the wife you always planned to have—the one your mother wanted for you, who she said was ideally suited to you—and my father will get his Lakaris grandson. And you will also get the next Lakaris heir to continue your bloodline.'

She swallowed again, felt razors in her throat.

'It's a happy ending all round,' she said.

Except for me.

She felt herself give a silent cry of anguish. But then it had never been going to be a happy ending for her, had it? And not just because of her father's ultimatum.

Because even with the merger Xandros would have terminated our marriage after six months. I would have lost him anyway. So what's the difference if that loss has happened sooner and I have to bear seeing my half-sister get the life that I would give everything to have…?

The pain was just the same.

She took another razored breath, feeling the torment of seeing Xandros again—parting from him again—knife through her.

Xandros was looking at her, his dark eyes holding hers. Yet suddenly they were veiled. Unreadable.

'The next Lakaris heir…'

His deep voice echoed hers. Something shifted in his eyes, in those dark, lambent depths. Something she could not recognise. She saw him take a breath, heavy and incised, and then he spoke again, his shoulders flexing minutely.

'Yes, well…' he said, and there was a heaviness in his voice that made no sense. 'That won't exactly be the case.'

Rosalie swallowed. 'I suppose Ariadne's baby might be a girl,' she heard herself reply—as if discussing its gender were just a passing topic of conversation, instead of a nail in the lid of the coffin of her stupid and pathetic hopes, a nail driven into her breaking heart.

'It can be anything it likes!' Xandros retorted.

Something shifted in his eyes again—something that seemed to ignite in them.

'Because it isn't mine.'

Rosalie could only stare, uncomprehending, feeling a flame deep within her that was like a searing point of light…a laser that shot with blinding brilliance.

She was staring at him, her face blank. It took all Xandros's strength to hold her gaze to tell her what she needed to hear.

'It would be a biological impossibility for it to be

so,' he went on, his eyes never leaving her gaunt, strained face.

He saw her face work.

'But the timing—your mother told me. Ariadne's into her second trimester, so her pregnancy must have begun while she was still…still engaged to you…'

His jaw steeled. 'Rosalie, why do you think Ariadne refused to marry me? I thought it was simply because she balked at doing her father's bidding. But there was another reason.' He took an incising breath, his mouth pressed tight. 'A reason I had already started to suspect, and which she has now confirmed to me. She met someone else. Someone who fathered her baby. There can be no doubt about it! Her baby *cannot* be mine, because the most I ever shared with your half-sister was a goodnight kiss!'

He looked at her. Her grey-green eyes were distended. Those eyes that had captivated him from the first—that still did. That always would…

'So now it's *you* who must see, Rosalie.'

But what *did* she see? What did this woman who had fled from him really see?

Too much and not enough.

He felt emotion crush his lungs. Emotion he needed to hold back.

'My mother got it wrong,' he said. 'Ariadne arrived out of the blue at the house, her pregnancy showing, and my mother jumped to what to her was the obvious conclusion. The *wrong* conclusion! When Ariadne realised what my mother had assumed she phoned me straight away. But it was too late.' His voice changed. 'You'd gone. Disappeared to London. Filed for divorce.'

He got up suddenly, striding restlessly to the window and back again, wheeling around to look down on her where she was sitting limply, immobile, white as a sheet.

'A completely unnecessary divorce,' he said quietly.

He saw the expression in her eyes change, saw something moving in them. And for the first time since Ariadne had phoned him at the airport in Thessaloniki he felt hope.

But then it was gone. And her voice, when she spoke, was as strained as it had been before, stumbling over her words.

'But it is still going to be necessary,' she said heavily. 'Our divorce. Because of what my father threw at me. His impossible demand that unless… Until…until I'm pregnant the merger you married me to get will never happen.'

He plunged his hands into his pockets. Steeled his jaw. Took a breath before saying what he had to say now.

'There won't be a merger,' he said. 'I'm pulling out of it.'

Xandros was looking at her. He was silhouetted against the drawn window drapes, hands plunged into his trouser pockets, his stance stiff, face expressionless. And yet in his eyes…

Rosalie felt a pulse start to thump in her throat. Hammering in her veins.

'You're pulling out?' she echoed, her voice as blank as her face. 'But *why*?'

'Why? Because I never…*never*…want you to doubt the reason I say this to you now.'

Something flashed across his face and the pulse at

her throat thumped more strongly yet. The set of his broad shoulders seemed different, somehow, but still tense.

'Why,' he asked slowly, his eyes never leaving her, 'do you call your father's demand "impossible"?'

She swallowed. There were still razor blades in her throat, drawing blood…

'Because…because…we were only meant to be married for half a year! My getting pregnant would have been a disaster!'

His eyes were resting on her…so dark. So unreadable.

'Would it?'

She stared. 'I don't understand…'

His expression changed. In place of that unreadable mask something moved in his eyes. Something it was impossible for her to read. Then the faintest smile hovered fleetingly at his mouth. The mouth that had once kissed her into senseless bliss but would never do so again.

Pain like an arrow across her cheek scathed her heart.

'Perhaps,' he was saying now, still speaking slowly, with the same strange expression in his face, 'I would have welcomed it.'

There was still the same tension across the broad sweep of his shoulders, in the motionless poise of his stance.

She felt her face pucker. 'Don't say that, Xandros—'

Her voice was broken. *She* was broken. Broken into tiny fragments that she could not hold together.

He stood looking down at her, that expression she could not read—dared not read—still in his eyes.

He was speaking to her again.

'Don't say it because the thought of bearing my child appals you? Don't say it because a child would bind us, one to the other, for all our days…all our lives? Don't say it because that would be a fate that would horrify you?'

She felt her throat twist, those razor blades embedded in it agonising. She could not stop them. Could not stop anything at all. Could not stop his voice—could not stop him starting towards her, hunkering down, taking her trembling hands in his. He was looking into her eyes, from which tears were starting to spill. Tears she could not bear to shed but could not stop.

'*Does* it appal you?'

His voice had changed, and she could not bear that either. Could not bear what it held…what it was asking of her.

'Don't tell me that it does! Don't tell me that!'

His eyes were holding hers now, and she could not stop that either—they were pouring into her.

'Because I won't believe you. Call me arrogant, conceited and presumptuous, but I won't believe you! I won't believe you, Rosalie, because my head is full of memories that give the lie to that! Memories that burn and scorch within me. Memories of the nights we have spent in each other's arms! Memories that glow with all the warmth and radiance of the summer sun. Memories of the days we have spent in each other's company. *Good* days…precious to me—so precious.' And now his voice was ragged with the emotion he was no longer trying to hold in check. 'Days I never want to end. Nights I never want to lose.'

His hands closed around hers, so warm, so strong, so comforting and protective. So possessive.

'You told me that you wanted to set me free,' he was saying now. 'But I don't *want* to be free of you! I don't *ever* want to be free of you!'

Her face was working, and inside her heart was working, too. 'You…you said… We agreed…when we married…six months…to get the merger done…'

He crushed her hands with his. Strong and warm and enclosing.

'I've told you—to hell with the merger! I don't want it any more!' His voice was vehement, then urgent. 'Because there is only one thing I *do* want.'

He lifted her hands to his mouth and kissed them, one after another, his gaze pouring into her like velvet.

'I wanted to tell you before you fled back to London. To tell you that our time together has changed me—changed me completely!' He made a face, half-rueful, half-wry. 'Rosalie, I freely confess that one of the main attractions of keeping our marriage temporary—of keeping *you* temporary—was the fact that it had been the way I'd always lived my life. It suited me.'

The rueful expression deepened.

'It suited me very well. So well it made me reluctant to agree to marry Ariadne, even though—as my mother and your father were so keen to point out—it would have been so "suitable". The relief I felt when she jilted me only confirmed that I was not ready to settle down. But what I was too blind to realise—' and now there was more than ruefulness in his voice…there was a twist of pain and remorse that caught at her as he spoke '—was how everything would change…with *you*! With *you* in my life! Day after day. Night after night.

Just *being* with you.' His expression changed again, and now there was a blaze in his eyes. 'Just you…making everything *wonderful*!' he said.

He kissed her hands again, keeping them fast in his as if he would never let them go again. His face was blurring in her vision now, and she could not breathe…dared not…could only gaze at him, listen to him speak…her heart so full she thought it must overflow with hope, with longing to hear what he was telling her…confessing…

He was speaking again now, and she clung to his words…to the hands holding hers so close, so fast…

'I was starting to feel it more and more. I was even welcoming the delays your father was putting in my way because they would give me more time with you! But I still never realised *why* I was feeling it—or what it was that I was feeling! It took that last weekend on Kallistris, seeing Maria and Panos's grandchildren, to open my eyes to what I truly wanted. Not the promise of my old freedom! What use would that be to me when my old life had gone for ever? I didn't want it back! What I wanted…' his voice softened '…was what I already had—with you. *Only* with you. You in my life, just as we were—for always. And more.' He took a breath. 'Children. A family…' He paused. 'A wife to love and be loved by…' He paused again. '*You*, Rosalie. Only you.'

Her tears were falling openly now, sliding down her paper-white cheeks. He brushed them away with his mouth softly, like velvet, and then his lips found hers, soft and quivering, and he kissed them, too.

'Only you,' he said again.

He drew back, his eyes full with all that he had said.

'I wanted you to come and join me in Thessaloniki—wanted you to start to discover *your* feelings just as I was discovering mine. I was starting to think about not wanting our marriage to end—wanting to make it permanent in the most binding way of all. Then Ariadne phoned, telling me that of all bitter ironies you believed she carried my baby—her, the very last person I would want to be the mother of my child now that I'd realised there was only one woman I could ever think to have a child with, to spend my life with! And everything exploded in my face!'

He gave a shudder, his face convulsing.

'Being without you these two endless weeks has been agony!' He shook his head, his eyes filled with remembered pain. 'Proving to me just how much you've come to mean to me! I've been *desperate* for you, Rosalie! Desperate to find you—desperate to tell you the truth. Not only the truth that my mother had got it so wrong about Ariadne, but the most important truth to me of all! That I love you and want you, beyond all things, to come back to me. To make our marriage real—and for ever.'

His gaze was pouring into hers again, his dark eyes turning to liquid gold. Turning her to liquid gold as well.

'Can you…? Will you…?' His voice was husky. 'Do you want that, too? Can you love me as I have come to love you? I won't give up hope, Rosalie! Ask of me anything but that!'

He gazed at her, drinking her in. His expression had changed again. Intensity and ardour softened it now, making it tender. Cherishing. Loving…

'The fact that you are sitting here with tears pouring

down your face from those eyes that have beguiled me since I first beheld them, and that you have let me kiss you as I have, and that your hands, Rosalie, are clutching mine as if you would never let them go… All that, my dearest heart, gives me cause to hope…'

She gave a choke—a cry from her throat. 'I didn't mean to fall in love with you, Xandros! Because I knew that wasn't what you wanted! It was no part of why we married. We were always destined to part! So…' She took a ragged breath, so much emotion inside her. 'Do you really mean what you have just said?'

His hands tightened on hers and he gave her an old-fashioned look before getting to his feet, retaining her hands, which he lifted with his.

'There may be only one way to prove myself,' he said, and the glint in his eyes was pure gold.

He drew her to her feet, her limbs unresisting. Her tears were drying on her cheeks and her vision was clearing. She was focussing on the one man alone she would ever want. The man who was now lowering his mouth to hers…

His kiss was everything she remembered—everything she would remember all her days for the searing joy that filled her as his mouth claimed hers. As his heart claimed hers. As *he* claimed her.

'My for ever wife,' he said, breathing in the sweet breath of her honeyed mouth. 'My for ever love.'

She gave herself to his kiss, long and sweet and deep, and her hands slipped from his to wind about his neck as his hands clasped her waist, holding her so close against him that nothing could ever part them again…

Except the buzzing in her apron pocket.

He pulled back. 'What the—?'

Rosalie gave a shaky laugh. 'It's my manager—wanting to know why I'm taking so long to turn down the bed in this room.'

Xandros yanked the phone from her pocket and answered it.

'This is Xandros Lakaris in Room 504. Mrs Rosalie Jones Lakaris is otherwise engaged right now. And for the next fifty years and more! Oh, and by the way, she's just handed in her notice. Effective immediately.'

He chucked the phone on the desk. Turned back to her. Took her into his arms again.

'I think,' he said, and there was a gleam in the liquid gold of his eyes that melted her, 'we can turn down this bed perfectly well together...'

He drew her down with him and she gave a sigh of bliss.

Of radiant, everlasting love and perfect, perfect happiness.

EPILOGUE

ROSALIE SMILINGLY ACCEPTED the glass of champagne that her mother-in-law's stately butler was offering to her from a silver platter before discreetly withdrawing. She and Xandros had just arrived from yet another sojourn on Kallistris, where they loved to spend all the time they could. But this was an occasion she would not have missed for all the world.

She raised her flute to the young woman sitting opposite her in the beautifully appointed drawing room, tenderly holding her newly christened baby in her arms.

It was Xandros who gave the toast, standing beside Rosalie's silk-upholstered armchair.

'To my sister-in-law and her beautiful daughter,' he said, raising his glass.

His words were echoed by his wife and his mother.

'To dear Ariadne,' his mother said fulsomely.

'To my wonderful sister!' Rosalie exclaimed warmly.

Her eyes met Ariadne's. In the months since she had returned to Athens, her heart soaring with happiness, so much had happened—and everything was wonderful… beyond wonderful!

Xandros's mother had greeted her with tears, asking

forgiveness for having caused so much grief, so unintentionally.

'I did not know you loved my son,' she had said. 'Or he you. I did what I thought I had to do—had no choice but to do—but I *never* meant you any harm, nor the grief I caused you! And now, if you can forgive me, I welcome you to our family as I should have done from the beginning—for you are a part of us for all time. You have made my beloved son the happiest of men, and for that you will always be precious to me.'

And it was her mother-in-law who had overseen the meeting between the two half-sisters. Rosalie had been full of trepidation, lest her hopes not be matched, but her fears had been unnecessary.

So like herself—yet so unalike—Ariadne had been eager in her greeting.

'You can't know how wonderful it is to have a sister!' she had exclaimed.

For a few moments Rosalie let her thoughts go to the man who had brought about the two half-sisters in their very different lives. Then she left him where he was—in his callous, uncaring existence. He had given love to neither of his daughters and neither of their mothers—he deserved nothing.

Her mouth twisted. For all that, her father would now get the only thing he seemed to want. Which, in turn, would give Xandros the merger which she had persuaded him not to withdraw from after all.

She needed no proof that Xandros wanted what she herself so longed for, for no other reason than the one they shared. A baby to bless their marriage and fill their cup of happiness to the brim.

Her eyes went now to Xandros, exchanging a secret

glance with him. They would not steal Ariadne's moment now, but very soon her own pregnancy would start to show, and then it would be a time for family rejoicing.

So she raised her glass again, her expression warm, and felt Xandros's hand on her shoulder warm upon her, cherishing and loving. How blessed she was to have so much!

Oh, Mum, you're the only one I miss who should be here—but you will be in my heart always, and in my memories. And if my baby is a girl I will give her your name—and all the love you gave to me.

Then her gaze went to her husband's once again, her heart overflowing as their eyes wound into each other's. Unconsciously her hand slipped to her stomach, fingers splaying in a protective gesture.

A little gasp came from her half-sister. Ariadne's eyes widened.

'Rosalie! Can it be…? I know that gesture! Are you—?' Her voice was breathless, excited.

Rosalie gave a helpless laugh, exchanging a rueful glance with Xandros. So much for secrecy!

Her mother-in-law had gone very still, her champagne flute poised halfway to her mouth, eyes only on Rosalie, bright with eager hope.

'Shall we?' Xandros asked of Rosalie, with resigned humour in his voice.

She gave a nod. Too late now for prevarication.

Xandros duly raised his glass again. 'I think,' he said, taking a breath, 'we have another toast to make… To the next Lakaris!'

There was a cry of delight from her mother-in-law, of excited glee from Ariadne, and then Xandros's smiling mouth was swooping down on hers in celebration, in joy, and in endless love.

As it always would be between them.

For all time. And way beyond.

* * * * *

If you fell in love with
The Greek's Penniless Cinderella
you're sure to adore these other stories
by Julia James!

Heiress's Pregnancy Scandal
Billionaire's Mediterranean Proposal
Irresistible Bargain with the Greek
The Greek's Duty-Bound Royal Bride

Available now!

COMING NEXT MONTH FROM

HARLEQUIN

PRESENTS

Available September 15, 2020

#3849 A BABY ON THE GREEK'S DOORSTEP

Innocent Christmas Brides

by Lynne Graham

When a tiny baby is left on his doorstep, billionaire Tor Sarantos can't believe his eyes. He's even more stumped when a beautiful woman arrives in a panic, declaring it's their son!

#3850 PENNILESS AND SECRETLY PREGNANT

by Jennie Lucas

Leonidas Niarxos is responsible for the death of Daisy's father. He's also the father of her child! Pregnant and penniless, Daisy must marry him for the sake of their baby, but will she forgive him before they say "I do"?

#3851 THE BILLIONAIRE'S CINDERELLA CONTRACT

The Delgado Inheritance

by Michelle Smart

Damián Delgado needs Mia Caldwell to act as his girlfriend for one weekend to save his business. Only, their intoxicatingly real connection is making it harder to believe it's all just pretend...

#3852 CHRISTMAS IN THE KING'S BED

Royal Christmas Weddings

by Caitlin Crews

Orion is determined to rule his once-dissolute kingdom with integrity and respect. That means honoring his betrothal to Lady Calista Skyros. A woman whose father deals in scandal—and who threatens his unwavering self-control...

#3853 THEIR IMPOSSIBLE DESERT MATCH

by Clare Connelly

A chance encounter between Princess Johara and a mystery lover was the perfect night. Until she discovers the man was her family's bitter enemy! Now Johara must travel to Sheikh Amir's desert palace to broker peace...and try to resist their forbidden temptation!

#3854 STEALING THE PROMISED PRINCESS

The Kings of California

by Millie Adams

Prince Javier de la Cruz's goal was simple. Tell heiress Violet King she's promised in marriage to his brother. His first problem? She refuses. His second problem? Their instant, unwelcome and completely forbidden chemistry!

#3855 HOUSEKEEPER IN THE HEADLINES

by Chantelle Shaw

Betsy Miller was ready to raise her son alone after tennis legend Carlos Segarra dismissed their night of passion. Now that the headlines have exposed their child, Carlos is back and everyone's waiting to see what he'll do next...

#3856 ONE SCANDALOUS CHRISTMAS EVE

The Acostas!

by Susan Stephens

Smoldering Dante Acosta has got to be physiotherapist Jess's sexiest client yet. Even injured, the playboy polo champion exudes a raw power that makes Jess giddy...but can she depend on him fighting for their chemistry this Christmas?

SPECIAL EXCERPT FROM

HARLEQUIN

PRESENTS

Orion is determined to rule his once-dissolute kingdom with integrity and respect. That means honouring his betrothal to Lady Calista Skyros. A woman whose father deals in scandal—and who threatens his unwavering self-control...

Read on for a sneak preview of
Caitlin Crews's next story for Harlequin Presents,
Christmas in the King's Bed.

"Your Majesty. Really." Calista moistened her lips and he found himself drawn to that, too. What was the matter with him? "You can't possibly think that we would suit for anything more than a temporary arrangement to appease my father's worst impulses."

"I need to marry, Lady Calista. I need to produce heirs, and quickly, to prove to my people the kingdom is at last in safe hands. There will be no divorce." Orion smiled more than he should have, perhaps, when she looked stricken. "We are stuck. In each other's pockets, it seems."

She blanched at that, but he had no pity for her. Or nothing so simple as pity, anyway.

He moved toward her, taking stock of the way she lifted her head too quickly—very much as if she was beating back the urge to leap backward. To scramble away from him, as if he was some kind of predator.

HPEXP0920

The truth was, something in him roared its approval at that notion. He, who had always prided himself on how civilized he was, did not dislike the idea that here, with her, he was as much a man as any other.

Surely that had to be a good sign for their marriage.

Whether it was or wasn't, he stopped when he reached her. Then he stood before her and took her hand in his.

And the contact, skin on skin, floored him.

It was so...*tactile*.

It made him remember the images that had been dancing in his head ever since he'd brought up sex in her presence. It made him imagine it all in intricate detail.

It made him hard and needy, but better yet, it made her tremble.

Very solemnly, he took the ring—the glorious ring that in many ways was Idylla's standard to wave proudly before the world—and slid it onto one of her slender fingers.

And because he was a gentleman and a king, did not point out that she was shaking while he did it.

"And now," he said, in a low voice that should have been smooth, or less harshly possessive, but wasn't, "you are truly my betrothed. The woman who will be my bride. My queen. Your name will be bound to mine for eternity."

HPEXP0920

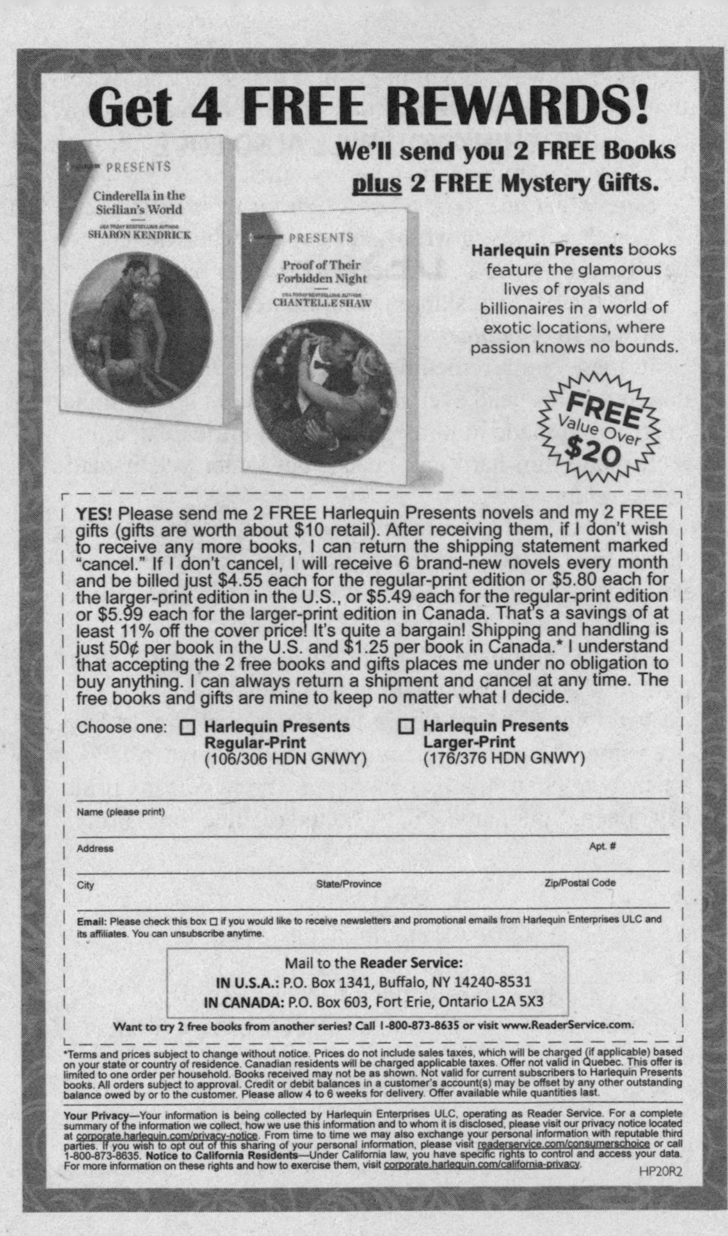
Get 4 FREE REWARDS!
We'll send you 2 FREE Books
plus 2 FREE Mystery Gifts.
PRESENTS
Cinderella in the Sicilian's World
SHARON KENDRICK
PRESENTS
Proof of Their Forbidden Night
CHANTELLE SHAW
Harlequin Presents books feature the glamorous lives of royals and billionaires in a world of exotic locations, where passion knows no bounds.
FREE
Value Over
$20
YES! Please send me 2 FREE Harlequin Presents novels and my 2 FREE gifts (gifts are worth about $10 retail). After receiving them, if I don't wish to receive any more books, I can return the shipping statement marked "cancel." If I don't cancel, I will receive 6 brand-new novels every month and be billed just $4.55 each for the regular-print edition or $5.80 each for the larger-print edition in the U.S., or $5.49 each for the regular-print edition or $5.99 each for the larger-print edition in Canada. That's a savings of at least 11% off the cover price! It's quite a bargain! Shipping and handling is just 50¢ per book in the U.S. and $1.25 per book in Canada.* I understand that accepting the 2 free books and gifts places me under no obligation to buy anything. I can always return a shipment and cancel at any time. The free books and gifts are mine to keep no matter what I decide.
Choose one: ☐ Harlequin Presents Regular-Print (106/306 HDN GNWY)
☐ Harlequin Presents Larger-Print (176/376 HDN GNWY)
Name (please print)
Address
Apt. #
City
State/Province
Zip/Postal Code
Email: Please check this box ☐ if you would like to receive newsletters and promotional emails from Harlequin Enterprises ULC and its affiliates. You can unsubscribe anytime.
Mail to the Reader Service:
IN U.S.A.: P.O. Box 1341, Buffalo, NY 14240-8531
IN CANADA: P.O. Box 603, Fort Erie, Ontario L2A 5X3
Want to try 2 free books from another series? Call 1-800-873-8635 or visit www.ReaderService.com.
*Terms and prices subject to change without notice. Prices do not include sales taxes, which will be charged (if applicable) based on your state or country of residence. Canadian residents will be charged applicable taxes. Offer not valid in Quebec. This offer is limited to one order per household. Books received may not be as shown. Not valid for current subscribers to Harlequin Presents books. All orders subject to approval. Credit or debit balances in a customer's account(s) may be offset by any other outstanding balance owed by or to the customer. Please allow 4 to 6 weeks for delivery. Offer available while quantities last.
Your Privacy—Your information is being collected by Harlequin Enterprises ULC, operating as Reader Service. For a complete summary of the information we collect, how we use this information and to whom it is disclosed, please visit our privacy notice located at corporate.harlequin.com/privacy-notice. From time to time we may also exchange your personal information with reputable third parties. If you wish to opt out of this sharing of your personal information, please visit readerservice.com/consumerschoice or call 1-800-873-8635. Notice to California Residents—Under California law, you have specific rights to control and access your data. For more information on these rights and how to exercise them, visit corporate.harlequin.com/california-privacy.
HP20R2